LYING
BENEATH

THANKS FOR
EVERYTHING — LOVE
THE FINAL PRODUCT !

ISBN-13: 978-0-9843096-3-4
ISBN: 0-9843096-3-2

www.aninkmover.com

LYING BENEATH

BENEATH

THE AURA OPERATION SERIES

KEVIN MORAN

ONE

Uncovering a Mystery

Ayla peered through the small crack between the door and the cold concrete floor, watching for the man with the gun. She panted and waited, sweat dripping down her forehead. Lying beside her, Derek looked back and held a finger to his lips. The man jogged in their direction, and Ayla held her breath.

He strode down the empty sidewalk, looking through the sight on his gun. Ayla squinted and tried to distinguish between the man's blurry outline and the dark, shadowy buildings. As she squirmed to get a better view, the rough concrete rubbed against her exposed skin. She inched her hand toward her backpack and reached for her camera. Derek turned, wide-eyed, and shook his head, emphasizing the finger against his lips.

Ayla ignored her boyfriend's concerns, and with one hand, she swung her camera around and pointed the lens through the sliver of an opening—just enough for part of her lens to focus on the man. She adjusted a few settings and pushed the shutter button. The camera clicked, and the sound echoed off the walls of the empty building. The man continued walking straight ahead, unfazed by the faint noise.

Ayla exhaled.

It was too good of an opportunity to pass up. She looked at the screen and studied the blurry picture of their hostile follower, then returned her attention to real life and watched the man draw closer to their building. His clothes were gray, with a small splash of green near his shoulder, and he wore a utility belt around his waist.

She held her breath again as he approached.

His boots crunched the gravel an arm's length away from the metal door.

Ayla closed her eyes, knowing it wouldn't make her invisible but hoping anyway. She pictured grain fields and tall oak trees in hopes of taking the focus away from the grit pressing against her skin, the stinging sweat in her eyes, and the tickle starting to form in the back of her throat.

The man stepped closer and stopped with his back to her. Barely visible from the cracked door, he shifted his boots in the gravel, sending a few rocks flying.

Ayla turned to Derek. His jaw was clenched, and a vein protruded from his neck. His face grew even redder, and his sweat dripped onto the concrete, adding to the stagnant pools of water in the neglected-building-turned-temporary-hideout. His eyes never once left the man just on the other side of the cracked-open door.

The gravel beneath the man's boots crunched again, and he

took off running in another direction. Ayla watched from under the door. The man's shadowy presence diminished in the distance until it eventually blended in with the city's surroundings.

She sighed. "Do you think we lost him?"

"Shh." Derek slammed his finger into his lips again, face redder than before, vein still popping out of his neck.

Ayla sighed at her boyfriend's ultra-conservative cautiousness, but she trusted his military training more than her instincts. After a few more minutes and a few more itches going unscratched, she couldn't stay silent any longer.

"Who do you think he was?" After reaching down to scratch her legs, she used her elbow to prop herself up. She punched a few buttons to make her camera screen come to life and flipped through pictures.

"Ex-military. A little odd to see him protecting abandoned buildings though." Derek stayed on his stomach, peering under the door. Ayla stared at her recent photographs and Derek's words turned into mumbles. She was lost in thought and didn't see Derek stand up until he spoke again. "Was it worth it?"

"These are great," she replied, standing up and following Derek.

"Better be." He walked around the perimeter of the building. "I can protect you from stray cats and homeless people, but once you throw in armed guards, we have a problem."

"You could just bring *your* gun." Ayla pointed the camera at him and made a pistol sound effect.

"Funny." He covered the lens with his hand.

"I'm just saying . . ." She panned her camera around. "This building might be better than any of the others we were in to-night, anyway." Light from the full moon streamed in from two stories above, through the expansive windows, and lit up the inside of the long-forgotten building, which was mostly empty other than remnants of machines and workbenches spread throughout the large space. Ayla meandered, stepping over pieces of garbage and chunks of crumbled brick and concrete. Every now and then, a mouse scurried across the floor. The stacks of old wooden crates piled five high inspired her to snap her camera and send more flashes of light into the dark corners of the building.

"Hey." Derek strode toward her. "What are you doing?"

"Taking pictures," she said.

"Turn off the flash," he told her. "And let's try not to stay too long." Derek walked past the bolted and chained front door and eyed another door on the side of the building. It was boarded up and blocked off by split and cracked two-by-fours.

"Uh-huh." Ayla's focus shifted to the ceiling and the large windows encircling the upper floor. Some of the glass was cracked or had imperfect holes from rocks smashing through, and others were empty panes where glass used to be.

She snapped more pictures, following the rule of thirds, and focused on the beams of moonlight. She followed the light down the brick walls and moved her camera closer to the ground to take in the shadows scattered across the floor and bouncing through and around the slots of the wooden crates.

"Hey, come here," Ayla called out, focused on the floor but no longer looking through her lens.

"What?" Derek jogged her way.

"What's that?" Embedded in the concrete was a circular brass disc about the size of a CD. Derek stepped forward and

4

dragged his foot across the floor, clearing off debris and rubble and revealing more of the worn marker. The piece of brass was stuck less than an inch into the concrete and had a design on top.

"Probably an old capped water pipe or survey marker or something," Derek said. He and Ayla leaned in closer. There were three rings inside the round marker, each ring smaller than the last, like a bullseye target. Inside the smallest circle was a stylized five-point star.

Ayla zoomed in with her camera. "Aura," she said.

"What?"

"Aura. It says 'Aura.'"

"Aura?"

"A-U-R-A. Aura. All uppercase. Right in the middle." Ayla adjusted her settings again and zoomed in further.

"That's it?" Derek asked.

"Oh." Ayla's voice squeaked. "There's also a small number three.'"

"Three?" Derek asked.

"Just a three. Three . . . circles? I don't know." She took another picture.

Derek paced and watched the doors. "How about just three more minutes?"

"Hold on," Ayla said. "I think there's more." She reached down and poked around the marker with her finger. "Look."

Derek looked where she indicated. Ayla's fingernails were just long enough to slip beneath the outer ring. She squiggled her pointer finger underneath and pulled. The rings were all connected to each other and peeled away from the marker.

"Wait, wait, wait." Derek lunged and grabbed Ayla's hand. "We have no idea what this is." He stood up, bringing Ayla with him.

"Don't you want to find out?"

"I don't want to break anything."

"But look . . ." Ayla trailed off and pointed at the ground. Four thin lines had now appeared, forming a two-foot square around the marker. She dragged her feet over the lines and took a few more pictures. The concrete seemed to have split apart and separated from the ground. "Get out of the shot," she directed Derek, who was standing inside the newly uncovered square.

He stepped back. "I'm not sure about this."

"All right, just a second." Ayla knelt, continuing her photoshoot. "It looks like a trapdoor or something." Her voice bounced around inside the empty building.

A scratching came from the opposite corner, near the boarded-up door. Ayla stopped shooting and looked up.

"It's not safe," Derek said, grabbing her arm. "We need to leave."

"Just a sec." Ayla fired off a few more pictures. "Now we can go."

She whipped her camera over her shoulder and jogged with Derek back to the entrance. They both rolled underneath the door they had been hiding behind, the crack just barely large enough to accommodate them, and out into the cold autumn air. As they jogged back to their apartment, through back alleyways and piles of brightly colored leaves, Ayla's mind wandered, and she got dizzy imagining the different explanations for what they had come across.

"You know we're going back, right?" Ayla walked through the door of their small apartment. She reached down and petted Bella, their chocolate lab, who waited for them near the entryway, and set

6

her backpack on the kitchen table, which acted both as her workspace and an ironing board. She took out her camera and looked through the new pictures.

"Why would I want to risk my life like that again?" Derek followed her through the door and fumbled with the always-finicky deadbolt, trying to lock the door behind him.

"That wasn't risking life." Ayla turned and smiled at Derek as he hung up his jacket on the wall-mounted pegboard by the door. "That was living it."

Derek rolled his eyes. "We could have been shot."

"But we weren't."

"But we could have been," Derek insisted.

Ayla dreamed of running through open spaces and living how she wanted to, but Derek worried about everything and had to be prepared, his military upbringing shining through. Their conflicts happened a lot, but over the years, she had learned how to deal with them. She walked toward him and threw her arms over his shoulders.

"You need to relax. You're so uptight."

"I could be more uptight." Derek broke out of her grasp and pulled up a chair at the kitchen counter, which was currently acting as an extra storage shelf and a laundry hamper. "I'm not interested in getting chased by armed guards."

"Well, where's the fun in that?" Ayla flipped the camera screen toward Derek. "You're telling me you don't want to find out what *this* is?" The screen showed the trapdoor, moonlight glinting off the star-shaped emblem engraved in the center.

"It's interesting," Derek said. "But like I said, it's probably just an old survey marker or something. Not a big deal."

"And the weird trapdoor thing?" Ayla pressed on.

"An access hatch? I don't know. Probably nothing."

"Fine, then don't come next time."

"I didn't say I didn't want to come."

"That's what I heard."

"I just don't want you going out alone," Derek insisted.

Ayla took a step away from her boyfriend. "You think I need protection?"

"I think I don't want you to die trying to get cool photos."

Ayla stepped back again. "You don't like my pictures?"

"That's not what I meant." He dropped his head in his hands. "Look, I . . . think it's dangerous and better if I come with you."

"I don't need you to protect me, Derek."

"I'm not saying you need me to protect you, but going together would be a better idea."

"According to you."

"Yes," Derek said. The vein in his neck started to bulge again. "Tell me when you want to go, and we can figure it out."

Ayla sighed. "Fine."

"Maybe we find out who owns that building and get permission first." Derek might have meant the words as a question, but that wasn't how Ayla interpreted them.

"You want to ask for permission?" She had lost count of how many times Derek had lectured her about the risks of her urban photography explorations.

"It wouldn't hurt."

"I'll look into it," she lied and turned her back, rolling her eyes when Derek couldn't see her. She relaxed her shoulders, happy to play the negotiator, the role she had played for so long she wasn't sure if it was a role anymore or if it had become part of her personality. She turned her attention back to the display of her camera. "I just have to go back. That place was fascinating."

"If you say so." Derek got up and went to the kitchen.

"Yeah, well, even if it's just a plain old survey marker and access door, I'd like to find out."

"Want anything to eat?" Derek poked his head out from behind the old fridge door.

"It's almost midnight . . ."

"Is that a no?"

Ayla thought for a moment. "What do we have?"

"Ummm . . ." Derek paused. "Leftover meatloaf, some beans and rice . . ." He moved some things around in the fridge. "Ketchup, a couple of eggs . . ."

Ayla scrunched up her face and stuck out her tongue. "I'll pass. Maybe just water."

Derek pulled out the meatloaf and dropped a chunk of it on a paper plate. He maneuvered around Bella, who took up the entire kitchen when she was in it, and threw his plate in the microwave. He filled up a glass with tap water and handed it to Ayla.

"Thanks," she said and took a large sip. "You thought that guy was ex-military?"

Derek stared at the microwave. "The guy with the gun?"

"No, the other guy tonight." Ayla rolled her eyes again, this time in full view of her boyfriend. "Of course the guy with the gun."

"Hard to say." The microwave dinged, and Derek took the plate out and sat next to Ayla at the table. "He seemed well-trained, and that gun wasn't standard. I'd guess it was a for-hire job, private security probably, maybe for Union Station."

"I didn't think they gave those guys real guns."

"Sometimes." Derek took a bite of his meatloaf.

"I didn't quite get a clear picture of him, but I managed to snap this." She turned the camera to show him the screen. The dark and blurry image showed a figure with a gun and a few details of his clothes. "I'll try to lighten it up to see if I can bring out any more details. Not sure it matters, but it would be nice to know who we're dealing with before I—" Ayla caught herself. "Before *we* go back."

"Just tell me when you want to go." Derek locked eyes with her. "And please, at least pretend to find out who owns the building." He shoved another piece of dry meatloaf into his mouth.

Ayla sighed. "Fine."

"Thank you," Derek said, standing up, the meatloaf gone from his plate. He let Bella lick off all the crumbs. "I have to go to bed. Early day tomorrow."

"Yep, I'll be right there."

She flipped through the pictures again, pausing on the star-shaped design. Her mind danced around the possibilities. Derek didn't see beyond the survey marker, but she envisioned opening the rest of the trapdoor and finding a magical, mysterious world waiting to whisk her away from her cramped apartment and stressful jobs. She looked up. Bella stared at her, waiting for scraps of food Ayla didn't have. Ayla reached down and ran her hand through Bella's fur.

"I know, Bella. I still love you."

Bella whimpered.

Ayla looked around the room and tried to remember how lucky she was. She tried to remember where she came from and what lay ahead, but right now, she kept picturing the old abandoned building. The brass marker. The star engraving. Aura. The secret passageway. The unknown.

She turned back to her camera and stared and studied.

Ayla walked through the city neighborhood, tightly gripping the straps of her backpack. Her hair stood on end, and goosebumps crept up her arms with every gentle, cool breeze that swirled by. She had finished a double shift and Derek wouldn't be home for hours, giving her enough time to slip out, do some exploring, come back, and pretend like she was sleeping.

The glow of the moon illuminated the empty buildings, giving them a hint of life in the darkness. But with half of the streetlights broken, and the other half giving off less light than a nightlight, she couldn't see much. She reached her hand toward her backpack, wanting to grab the flashlight, but paused after realizing the attention of anyone, especially a guard with a gun, would ruin her plans.

With every step, she surveyed her surroundings like Derek had taught her. She paused for a moment to snap a few pictures of Union Station off in the distance. Most people came here for Union Station and ignored the surrounding buildings, which were dimly lit by scattered window lights here and there, dotting the black night sky.

To reach the building, she crossed a lot full of gravel and weeds and walked up to the old rolling dock they used to sneak in the night before. Tonight, she had time to examine the mysterious place.

Chunks of brick were falling off the exterior of the building.

What was left of the windows near the top was old and, she guessed, original to the building, which probably meant 1950s or earlier. An old wooden beam that was part of the original loading dock was splitting apart and falling off the concrete, like an old relic from history trying to hang on.

There were chips and dents scattered throughout the sidewalk, and the entire place called out for someone to bring along a tool belt and pay attention to it for once. The building was a perfect industrial setting for bustling workers loading and unloading whatever came off the docks at Union Station and then hauling things back and forth in a whirl of activity. If she closed her eyes, the sounds of work crews came alive: burly men scuffling around and tossing crates with ease between the busy loading dock and old diesel trucks.

Ayla stepped onto the loading dock. The rusting edges of the oversized metal door caught her eye, and she snapped a few pictures. She slung her camera back over her shoulder and nudged the door with both hands. Like the rest of the place, this door hadn't seen any attention in years, and it was rusted in place as if to say, "I give up. Just leave me be," so Ayla brushed her hands off and dropped to her knees.

She clutched her camera close against her chest, lay on her stomach, and rolled under the door like she had done the night before, but this time without the added pressure of being chased by a man with a gun. Once through, she sat up, dusted off her hair, checked her camera, and headed straight to the marker on the ground.

The stench of rat droppings, dirt, and stale water lingered heavy. Nothing had been touched since she and Derek had come through the night before. The outline of the trapdoor remained, and Ayla stepped inside the square.

"Aura," she said out loud, leaning down to examine the etching inside the circles. "What does it mean?"

She traced the outline of the trapdoor with her camera and focused on the seam in the floor. She set her camera down and ran her fingers along the edge of the outlined square, picking up dirt and debris along the way. Her fingers found their way to the brass rings inside the circular marker, and she slipped them through the loops again. She lifted the rings up, slowly, until she had enough room for both of her hands. She clutched the biggest ring and pulled.

Nothing happened.

She braced herself, counted to three, and pulled harder.

The door still didn't budge.

"Come on, Ayla," she said to herself. She set the ring down and brushed off her hands. To give her shoes a clean grip, she kicked dirt off the floor, and then she picked the ring back up and held it with both hands. Squatting over, she heard Derek's voice yelling "lift with your legs!" as she counted up in her head.

One.

Two.

Three.

She pulled, and nothing happened.

She let out a grunt.

She thought of her tiny apartment and small paychecks and pulled harder.

She thought of growing up without her father and pulled harder.

She thought about her mother in hospice and pulled even harder.

13

She pulled until she thought her arms would rip out of their sockets and send her flying across the room.

She kept pulling, and the dirt and buildup of decades of decay and neglect fell away from the concrete seams. Dust swirled in the air, causing the moonlight filtering through the windows to dance around the building like an old-fashioned disco ball.

The concrete gave way, and a chunk of the floor started to rise. Ayla slipped her hand under the now-freed door and let go of the ring. She lifted the heavy slab with both hands and swung it toward the wall on the hidden hinges holding it in place. She inched her way up the slab until it leaned against the side of the wall.

Ayla rested her hands on her knees and sucked in air. She now faced a dark hole in the floor and a small, wooden ladder leading to nothingness.

The newly revealed pit in front of her was black and empty, but it held so much hope that she had to restrain herself from immediately jumping down and proclaiming victory. A life of being stuck and wanting something more all led to this moment, a moment that held all the possibilities in the world. A change, *any* change, would be better than her daily grind of trying to support herself and her boyfriend and their little existence.

Derek's voice chirped in her head as if he were there. "It's not safe," he'd say, or "We should call the cops first." He didn't understand the lack of adventure and the feeling of meaninglessness engulfing her lately.

Her eyes drifted farther down the dark abyss and her mind wandered back to the cemetery a short three months ago. She'd had some time to prepare, but it hadn't been enough.

LYING BENEATH

* * *

She looked around at the people gathered, dressed in black, most with their heads hung low and staring at the ground. A lot of the people she knew, but some she didn't. A man with sandy hair, whom Ayla didn't recognize, stood next to their old neighbor, Mrs. Potts, who stood next to Stan, the grocery store owner from their hometown.

Stan brought his wife. They both looked sad and every now and then looked up and made eye contact with Ayla, but never for an extended period of time. In front of Stan was Mrs. Rodriguez, the director of the hospice home. Next to her was a man with dark hair, presumably her husband. The Rodriguezes were in a row with the rest of the staff from hospice.

"Thank you," Ayla said at the podium next to her mother's casket. "Thank you all for coming. Jake and I appreciate your support." She looked at her brother holding back tears. He was younger than her, about five years apart, from a different father. They had grown up together, them and their mother, fending for themselves, forming tighter-than-normal bonds. She always called him her whole-brother, because to her, he was more than a half-brother.

"I want you to know that my mother would love to see all of your smiling faces here." Ayla forced a smile. "And she'd want you to know you shouldn't be sad." Tears welled in her eyes. "She'd want you to be happy and to know you had an influence on her life. I know . . ." She pulled a tissue out of her pocket and dabbed her face, then paused and took a breath. "I know she's happy now, maybe happier than ever. And I hope everyone

here . . ." *She tilted her head and blew her nose away from the crowd. "I hope everyone here gets to see what my mom always saw: that life is meant to be lived and enjoyed. She worked impossibly hard . . ." Ayla's gaze caught Stan's. She blew her nose again. "And she raised Jake and me as best as she could. But at the end of the day, her time was cut short—" Ayla broke down in tears and didn't have enough tissues in her pocket, so she pulled her sleeve up to her face. Jake came forward from the crowd to comfort her. Their childhood priest, sitting in the first row, quickly took the podium.*

The last three months had been some of the worst in Ayla's life. Traveling to see her mom, making sure Jake was taken care of, taking responsibility for her mother's estate—or lack thereof—all while trying to work two jobs and keep her own head above water.

Her energy was drained just thinking about it. No amount of rest had been enough for her. She found herself stuck in a hamster wheel, constantly trying to catch up to be able to slow down. So far, in the past twenty-four hours, this little mystery in the abandoned building had been a great distraction. She grasped her backpack and stepped onto the ladder, holding onto the imaginative wonderlands and mysteries the dark void held.

Her foot rested on the first rung, and she tested the ladder's stability before committing her weight to it. She turned around and clutched the top of the ladder and cautiously slid one foot down to the next rung. *One step after another, slow and steady,* she reminded herself as she lowered herself beneath the floor.

Just before her head sank below floor level, she looked around to view the abandoned building one last time. As she took the final step, she found herself covered in darkness. Her pupils expanded with every step she took, one foot after another on her way down the ladder. The darkness engulfed her, and there was no way for her to know if she was close to the bottom or still near the top.

She remembered the flashlight in her backpack but didn't dare take her hands off the ladder, so she kept going. She went farther down, step after step, and tightened her grip with every rung. Sweat formed around her hairline, falling past her forehead and dripping off her nose. She paused, rested, and, after a minute of pure silence, gathered herself again and kept going.

Her shoe finally landed on a solid surface. She wriggled her foot around and planted it into the soft dirt. With both hands clinging to the old wooden ladder, she dropped her other foot to the ground. She freed one hand from the ladder and bent over, extending her hand to the ground. The cool dirt stung her palm like a frozen ice pack. She wiped the back of her hand across her forehead, trying not to smear dirt on her face.

Her eyes had adjusted to the darkness, but she couldn't see five inches in front of her. She reached into her backpack and grabbed her ancient flashlight. She switched it on and banged it a few times into the palm of her hand as the light flickered to life. Her line of visibility extended from five inches to five feet. She turned around, away from the ladder, and stared ahead at the confined, claustrophobic hallway.

It was colder than she expected, like stepping into a walk-in freezer, and it smelled like mold and dirt and wasn't any more pleasant than the building above. The walls matched the dirt of the floor, with wooden beams every two or three feet, probably for support.

The ceiling had a wooden-beam support structure, too, and was one foot higher than Ayla stood tall. Wiring hung off a timeworn light fixture near the ceiling. It was rusty and full of spiderwebs.

She inched forward, scanning the walls, the floor, and the ceiling for any signs of recent activity. There were no doors, windows, or any other openings. The dirt-floor hallway had only one direction to go, so on she went.

She walked for a while, slowly, with her flashlight leading the way. Her imagination ran wild with the possibilities of what lay ahead. If Derek were there, he would probably squash all her ideas and talk about access tunnels and whatnot, but Ayla let her mind wander into the unknown.

Her mind conjured up images of secret hideouts and speakeasies; she pictured people moving through the Underground Railroad and wondered if this was part of it. Vivid images of drug-smuggling rings and human trafficking jumped in and out of her mind. Anything was possible up ahead, past the reach of her flashlight.

It was exciting.

It was new.

It was different.

Ayla squinted as her flashlight reflected off something in front of her. She walked closer and soon found a beaten and bruised steel door. Her imagination took off again. She stopped walking and shined her flashlight across the door, revealing letters caked in dirt and dust.

Stamped onto the door was "WW-8." She found her camera in her bag and grabbed a few pictures of it, then walked up next to the door and ran her fingers across the bumpy engraving.

Her hands moved from the center of the door to its edges. She searched for any weaknesses or hinges but found none. Tapping her knuckles against the cold steel, she confirmed the door was solid. There was no handle or any other way of opening it. Her heart pounded and her mind spun.

I came all this way to be stopped by a door?

Her fingers crawled along the edges a second time. She clawed wherever the door allowed, hoping for a crack, a weakness, or something to grab. Her fingers stung with pain, and she decided to stop when they went numb—at least for now.

Thwarted by a solid steel obstacle, she turned off her flashlight and was engulfed by total darkness and crushing defeat.

"You went back?" Derek said, raising his voice.

"I had to."

"Without me?"

"Yes."

"Didn't we discuss this?"

"Derek, you don't—"

"Why would you do that?" His face turned red, and the vein in his neck popped out a few centimeters.

"I'm sorry. I just—"

"You could have gotten in serious trouble."

"But I didn't!" she blurted out. "I'm fine, Derek. Can you please listen—"

"No," Derek said. "I thought we had an understanding." He continued without letting her defend herself. "Did you try to get permission or find out who owns that building? Did you think about telling me? Did you take any protection? You could have gotten killed!"

"There were no guards—"

"That's not the point," he said. He sucked in a deep breath and started pacing.

Ayla stood silently, waiting for him to come to his senses. When his face turned less red and his breathing slowed, she spoke up, lowering her voice and trying to sound weak.

"I found a door . . ."

Derek stopped mid-stride. "A door?"

"Kind of," Ayla said, stronger this time. She fetched her camera from the kitchen and returned to Derek in the living room. "Come here." She sat on the couch that doubled as a guest bed, which also served as a dog bed. "The hatch on the floor was still cracked, just like we left it. I opened it up and there was a ladder leading down into the ground." Ayla scrolled backward in her pictures and found one showing the opening of the trapdoor.

"And you went in there?" The vein in Derek's neck threatened to break through his skin.

Ayla put her hand on his leg. "Yes, I went down the ladder. I'm fine, okay?"

Derek closed his eyes and took a deep breath. "Okay," he said.

"So, I get down there, and it looks like an old carved-out tunnel. Dirt floor, wooden beams holding up the place. I follow it for a bit, and then, out of nowhere, there's this metal door. I walk up to it and see 'WW-8' engraved on it." She found another picture, this time of the door, that highlighted the engraving.

Derek propped up the camera with one of his hands and looked at the screen. "Please don't tell me you went through that door."

"That's the thing: I couldn't. It was welded shut or something.

No drafts around the edges, no light from the other side—it was the weirdest thing."

"Let me see that picture again." Derek leaned in as Ayla angled the camera screen his way. "Are you sure it wasn't a plaque for something?"

"It *seemed* like it was meant to be a door. I'm not sure how to explain it, you know?"

"Why would 'WW-8' be engraved on a door?"

"I don't know. That's kind of weird, right?"

"Sounds like a plaque, not a door."

"Okay, say it is a plaque. What's it for? 'WW-8' . . ." She paused at the thought. "Maybe . . . Maybe it's nothing. I don't know. Why would anyone put a plaque under an old factory? Why the elaborate hatch door and engravings? I don't get it."

"Still could be an access hatch for something."

"Maybe it's something related to the 'Aura' engraving on that marker," Ayla said.

"You mean that survey point?"

"'Aura' and 'WW-8' don't seem to go together." Ayla ignored her boyfriend and kept thinking out loud. "Wild . . . window . . . welding . . ."

"Are you just naming W-words now?" Derek let out a slight laugh. "I don't think that's going to help. It could be anything."

"I know. I'm so confused."

They sat in silence, trying to fit the pieces together. Bella looked at them, trying to sleep on the small space they'd left for her at the end of the couch.

"We have to go back," Ayla finally said.

"I still can't believe you went without me," Derek replied. "Let's at least find out what we're dealing with. Maybe you've set off some alarm somewhere. Who knows?"

"Derek, I didn't see anyone when I went back. There were no mysterious men with guns, or triggered alarms, or—"

"That you know of," Derek cut in. "Look . . ." He slumped back into the couch. "I want you to be safe."

"I know." Ayla rested her head on his shoulder. "And I love that you worry about me so much. But, sometimes, it's okay to let go a little. Sometimes, it's okay to risk a few things."

"I know," Derek said. "I know. I've come so far. *We've* come so far. I mean, if you could tell our ten-year-old selves this is what our life is like now, do you think they'd believe us?"

Ayla had talked with Derek about this before. Their backgrounds included abusive or nonexistent fathers and whispers and gossiping behind their backs, and while it was in the past, their stories often found their ways to their everyday lives, for good and bad. It often brought them together, especially when things fell apart around them again.

"Probably not." Ayla stood up now. Bella jerked awake. "But you can't stop trying things now. If you *almost* got into a car accident once, you wouldn't stop driving forever, would you?"

Derek slouched in the couch. "We . . . We have a good thing here, and I'd like it to stay that way."

Ayla looked around their cramped apartment at their cheap, broken, second-hand furniture, their scuffed-up walls, the stained and discolored flooring, the water-marked ceiling, and, finally, back at Derek. "I love that I'm with you, and I love our life together, but don't you ever daydream about something else? Getting away, or going on an adventure? Anything to get . . . to get out?"

"Get out?" Derek looked confused. "Are you not happy?"

"No, no, I *am* happy. I couldn't be happier with you and Bella." Their dog looked up from the couch. Ayla sighed. "But, sometimes, with everything going on, and with us being in a tough spot financially, sometimes, I just get lost in thought. Especially lately with my mom and brother and everything going on . . ." She trailed off and looked at Derek. "You're saying you never fantasize about what a different life would be like?"

"I do, but I don't let that take away from my happiness today."

Ayla sighed again and threw her arms around Derek. "Me too," she said. "I love you."

"I will *always* love you." Derek kissed her forehead.

TWO

Into a New World

The mysterious door kept appearing in Ayla's head, and she found herself lying in bed and staring at the ceiling, thinking about it. Her gaze fluttered between their water-stained ceiling and Derek as she tried to think of anything other than the mysterious hole. After an agonizing, sleepless few hours, Ayla peeled back the sheets and slithered her way to the bedroom floor. She tiptoed around the full-sized bed and paused at the door. With her hand on the wooden doorframe, she looked back at Derek, who was unaware of the world around him and the stirring in Ayla's head. He would be mad, but she couldn't sit and wonder anymore. She tilted her head, smiled, blew a kiss, and tiptoed her way into the living room. To make sure Bella wouldn't bark, she walked up to her and patted her back to sleep.

"Good girl," Ayla whispered. She crept over to the table where she left her always-ready-to-go backpack and carefully slipped it over her shoulders. She stepped into her already-tied shoes and approached the finicky door. It squeaked and creaked. Ayla fiddled with the deadbolt, and when it finally let her out, she guided the door closed and headed out into the night. She was determined to find out what was beyond the mysterious door.

She reached the old building quickly but stopped mid-stride. The loading dock door wasn't cracked open like it had been before.

Was somebody here? Were they onto us? Was it the man with the gun? Was Derek right about the tripped alarm?

She crouched, looked around, and made her way to the loading dock ledge. She paused against the cold concrete, listened, and waited. The inside of the building seemed quiet, and no gravel crunching or boots stepping came from outside.

After coming this far, she wasn't going back now. An unwelcoming bolted and chained front door blocked her obvious way into the building, so she walked around the side to the opposite end, where she found a less intimidating door. This one had long since been boarded up.

Ayla pulled out a miniature crowbar from her backpack. She slipped one end of the bar behind the wood and, in one swift motion, yanked forward, causing the wood to give way. With the crowbar in one hand, she pried back the broken part of the wood. Behind the new crack was a shiny, metallic sheen. She leaned in closer and brought her flashlight up to her face.

Metal. Welded shut. A good alternative to a "Do Not Enter" sign.

For being an old, rundown, out-of-the-way building, it sure had its secrets. Ayla let the plywood slip back into place. She'd have to think of another plan.

She continued along the edge of the building until she turned the corner and faced the alleyway for this building and the one next to it. There was an old green- and rust-colored dumpster and a nonfunctioning streetlight.

Ayla's gaze continued up past the light post and back to the building, where she focused on a row of windows near the roof-line. The windows looked big enough to fit through. Growing up, she had climbed the giant trees in her neighborhood, but it had been a while. Though the path looked intimidating, she wasn't letting anything stop her tonight. She grabbed a handful of rocks from the street and shoved them into her pockets.

She pulled her backpack farther up her shoulders, made sure her hood was firmly secured and strapped to her head, grabbed the light post, and shimmied toward the windows. The slick streetlight was trickier to climb than the bark of oak trees, but after some patience and slippage, she reached the top.

She studied the old-style warped windows in front of her. From her pocket, she grabbed a few rocks and hurled them at the windows, which broke with little resistance. She shimmied on top of the light post, maintained her balance in a half-squatting position, and took a leap of faith toward the broken window. She grabbed onto the ledge and pulled herself up and through the steel frame of the window.

Once fully inside the building, she sat on the window ledge and got her bearings. She worked her way down the wall a bit until her foot touched one of the piles of boxes. From there, she hopped down to the floor.

She was in.

Quickly, she found her way back to the emblem and open hatch in the corner of the room. Everything had remained untouched since her last visit. Whoever blocked off the entry points must not have counted on her finding another way in.

Ayla double-checked the supplies in her backpack: flashlight, cell phone, wallet, keys, crowbar, blanket, camera. She wasn't sure what to expect and wanted to be prepared in any scenario.

With her flashlight out, she shoved everything else back in, strapped and clasped her backpack, and soldiered into the open hatch. She gingerly took step after step on the old, wooden ladder, grasping the worn, splintered edges and counting her steps as she moved down. Twenty rungs stood between the top and the bottom, which seemed much shorter than the first time she took this journey.

She landed on the dirt and pointed her flashlight down the long, dark hallway and started counting her paces to the metal door. After thirty-seven and a half paces through the cobwebs, she found the mysterious door.

Thoughts of Derek's comments ran through her mind. "Are you sure it wasn't a plaque or something," he had said. She leaned in to inspect the metal. She knocked on it, three times, rapping her knuckles below the 'WW-8' engraving. She wasn't an expert, but it sounded like hollow space behind the door.

She kicked the bottom of the door a few times, each time increasing in strength and each time reconfirming her hollow space theory. She plucked the mini crowbar out of her backpack. Her fingers traced the edge of the metal sheet again, trying to find a gap. She plunged the crowbar into as many promising spaces as she could but found nothing more than wiggle room. She tried the top of the door, too, with about as much success.

After admitting defeat, she turned her back to the steel obstacle and lowered herself to the ground. She sat on the floor, dropped her crowbar to her side, and held her head in her hands. It killed her that this mystery haunted her, and all she could do was sit here and come up short, unable to figure out its secrets.

She curled her knees up to her chest. Derek wouldn't be happy, and she had felt a little crazy. Now that it was all for nothing, she felt even more worthless.

A large, heavy sigh escaped her lungs.

Her adventures would be few and far between, and this wasn't one of them. She slammed her fist into the door, sending a shock wave up her arm. It hurt, but she had grown numb to being stuck in the hamster wheel of life. She wanted nothing more than to start a new adventure with the man she loved, who was currently curled up in bed, blissfully unaware of the ongoing turmoil inside of her. She loved him and wanted to tell him again, as she now sat alone at the end of a dark, dingy, dead-end hallway, feeling as small as she ever had.

She was enticed but trapped.

She was intrigued but exhausted.

She clenched her fists and gritted her teeth.

She yelled at the empty space in front of her, picked up the crowbar by her side, and jammed it into the space between the door and the ground.

Something threw off her balance, like someone had kicked her back support out from behind her, and she clawed at the dirt walls to keep from falling. She turned around and stood. The door, her nemesis, had vanished, and in its place was a wall made of a substance with the consistency and color of strawberry jam. It was shiny and gooey and, by far, the strangest-looking wall she had ever seen. She staggered backward and nearly fell, too, but caught herself in time. The intimidating, eerie wall stood there, silently staring at her.

It mocked her.

It dared her.

Is this real?

She inched forward with her flashlight, getting closer to the gel-like wall. An inch away, she paused and held her breath as she pushed the flashlight forward, sinking it into the wall. The light around her subsided, leaving the faint red glow of the wall. She pulled her flashlight back out and inspected it. It seemed fine. She turned it on and off, and it still worked like a normal flashlight.

Am I hallucinating?

She shook her head and took a couple of deep breaths to regain her composure. After begging for adventure and experiences, she finally faced the unknown and had second thoughts. She dropped her gloves and forced herself to take a step forward, her hand held out, shaking on its way to the wall. She pushed it through the gel-like substance and gasped for air.

Nothing happened. Her hand felt the same as it always had. She pulled it back from the wall, turned it over, and wiggled her fingers to make sure they still worked.

I'm crazy.

She didn't want to turn back and face reality.

She didn't want to turn back to the comfortable and the known.

This was exactly what she asked for, and she knew she had to keep going.

With one more deep breath, she stood tall and walked through the wall.

* * *

The cold feeling rushing through Ayla's body started to subside, and the tingling sensation throughout her skin slowed until it left entirely. She touched her face and checked for blood, then made sure her body parts were all intact.

Her flashlight lit up an unfamiliar stairwell that spiraled farther underground in front of her. She spun around in time to see the red glow of the jelly, gooey wall receding behind the closing door. She lurched forward and jammed her hand against the metal, trying to slow it down, but to no avail. The door slammed shut. She was face to face with the engraved letters at the top. "WW-8." The only difference here was a mix of random numbers and letters below the bold engraving.

What is this?

Her eyes widened as she inhaled quickly, and she scurried to her bag and tried to find her crowbar. She scattered the contents on the floor, lit them up with her flashlight, and searched through them, sending dust and debris through the beams of her light. She froze and stared up at the door. The crowbar was on the other side, on the ground, next to her gloves.

She banged on the door and cried out, hearing nothing but the response of her echo bouncing off the walls. Her heart rate skyrocketed, and she couldn't tell if it was panic or adrenaline at the thrill of a new adventure she had been desperately seeking.

Her eyes widened even more, and she swung the flashlight around, looking for other routes of escape. She turned around to face the stairwell again; it was her only hope.

She paused and tried to collect herself.

Her heart slowed, and her breathing returned to normal. She grabbed her backpack and took a step toward the stairs.

Chunks of the stairs were missing, cobwebs encased the splintered, wooden railing, and the exposed light bulbs following the stairs were mostly dead or flickering on the edge of existence. The steel treads on the steps were rusted out in most places, with trash scattered around the small landings, and mouse droppings covered a majority of the surfaces. The stench matched that of the dumpster at the restaurant Ayla worked at and was all too familiar with.

She stepped around the landmines of mouse feces until she reached the first step. A large portion of the step was gone, so Ayla settled her foot near the edge and slowly transferred her weight onto it. She tested the support, rocking back and forth. The step held her weight, so she exhaled and moved onto the next one.

It was a slow process. At each landing she paused for a breath before carrying on. Each level down brought dimmer light bulbs and what felt like a five-degree drop in temperature. It was dark and damp and smelled like mildew, but she kept going. Sheer will propelled her body forward, like her brain had shut off but her body kept moving.

She hadn't done anything quite as crazy as this in her life, and as her flashlight started becoming the only source of light, her heartbeat increased again, and sweat dampened her back and rolled down her temples.

Step after step, down she went.

After twelve landings, she lost count. All the agonizing real-life situations were a dozen stories above her now. She dropped the tension in her shoulders and neck and relaxed. She only had to focus on the next step in the stairwell, not the next step in her life.

She breathed in, foot down.

She breathed out, foot down.

Down she went, farther and farther.

Ayla climbed down and down until there were no more steps in front of her. Where the stairs should have been on this landing, there was a lone door. A standard, old-fashioned wooden door. There were no mysterious markings or odd letters and numbers, just a door with an old brass knob. Ayla turned it, and the door opened.

She slowly pushed the door open, and instead of a solid floor like she expected, there was an open, wire-framed, catwalk-style walkway. The metal was newer than the stairs she had just descended and didn't have rust or missing chunks.

Under the catwalk, bright lights projected onto workspaces with tables and empty chairs, computers, and a collection of other electronic-looking things Ayla didn't recognize. She opened the door farther, all the while watching the empty room one story below her.

Ayla squeezed through the opening in the door, careful not to open it any wider. The loud noise and heat hit her all at once. It was like an overworked furnace whirring away in a utility closet. She adjusted to the change in temperature and volume, secured her backpack, and tiptoed out onto the catwalk. She studied the room below her.

There were computers—those she recognized—but there were also scattered and unfamiliar electronics along the tables and floor. There were white cloth tarps here and there, sometimes covering things, other times seemingly thrown on the tiled floor at random.

She crawled forward. She didn't see any people, only doors and windows that looked like they were leading to another room or hallway and an occasional uncomfortable-looking chair.

One hand at a time, she kept crawling. Her body switched to autopilot, and her brain actively searched for and assessed threats below. Derek would be proud.

She moved across the room and found that the catwalk and false ceiling extended into other rooms. She crept forward. The far wall was thick, a good two or three feet. When she came upon the next room, she peered into it. A bald, pale man in a lab coat occupied one of the chairs, clicking away at a computer.

Her fingers clamped down on the catwalk steel and she watched the man walk over to a table in the corner. He placed a spherical object inside what looked like a bowl of green Jell-O in the middle of the table. After walking back to his computer, he hit some keys. The man stopped and looked back at the table. A short zapping sound came from somewhere, and the ball bobbed up and down in place. It eventually came to a stop, and after a few seconds of looking over the computer screen, the man got up and walked to the door. He opened it, and she leaned forward to get into a better position to hear him.

"What about that time? I . . ." The door closed behind him.

This was Ayla's opportunity. She crept across the catwalk, trying to reach the other side of the room. She turned around and grabbed a quick glance at the ball. It seemed ordinary, like one Bella would play with at the park.

The man came back in through the door, muttering something that sounded like "let's see" and sat back down at the computer. Ayla was now in the same corner as the ball. She leaned over and poked her head out to glance at the experiment going on below her. The man typed something into the computer again, then turned his stare at the ball in the corner of the room. The zapping sound fired up again, but Ayla didn't have a chance to see what happened after that.

A shooting pain hit her head like a cluster headache, and she slumped onto the catwalk. She was conscious enough to know that she made a loud *thud* when her body hit the steel. She grabbed at her head and winced in pain.

"Hey!" the man called out, now looking up at the ceiling. "What are you doing up there?"

Ayla couldn't speak but wasn't sure she wanted to, anyway. She was disoriented and wasn't sure which way she had come from. Once she'd staggered to her feet, she picked a direction and started stumbling down the walkway. Each footstep against the hardened steel sent another warning sign to the rooms below. She lumbered past more rooms and tried to get her bearings.

Her heart beat faster.

She panted.

Her vision started to tunnel in and spin faster.

At the end of the walkway, she found the door she thought she had come through. She grasped the doorknob and pulled. The door didn't budge, so she tried again, bracing herself against the floor. Even with all her weight behind it, nothing seemed to want to go her way.

There was a ladder off to the side, like the fire escape from their apartment. She jumped over the railing and grabbed on. She rappelled down, landing on the tile below.

For a brief second, she paused, trying to catch her breath and shake off her light-headedness. Derek was right, and she regretted not making sure he was with her. This could have all been prevented if he were here, but it was too late. Her only hope now was that he'd know what to do when he woke up.

She took a deep breath and sprinted down the hallway. There were doors and windows and blurs as she flew past them, distancing herself as much as she could. A set of double doors opened for her, and she sped through them, stumbling into a bigger room with tables and people. Startled by the new, blurry, people-like shapes, she fell, then scrambled back onto all fours, trying to head back to where she had come from.

The outlines of people approached her, and as they got closer, the blurry lines became more focused.

A faceless man stepped forward.

He mumbled. It sounded like he was under water.

Ayla tried to speak, but her lips were stuck together and her jaw was frozen.

She collapsed onto the floor.

The last thing she remembered was the faceless man leaning over her crumpled body.

There were weird sounds.

Rushing sounds, like she was standing under a waterfall.

The lights were blurry. And white.

Ayla didn't know if she was dead or alive, in heaven or still on Earth.

The blurry shapes came into focus.

The white lights continued whizzing by.

She was lying on a cart of some kind and being wheeled down

a hallway. The rushing noises around her were voices, people running alongside the bed, mostly talking to each other. The people pushed her through a door and into a room. More shapes came into focus now, and Ayla tried to look around. There was a big bed in the middle of the room. She was wheeled next to it and lifted onto the center.

She winced at a grating pain slamming into her forehead, so she closed her eyes until the pain subsided. When she felt better, she looked around and tried to take in her surroundings.

Anonymous people wearing protective hazmat suits filled the room. They were like an army of white-colored bees buzzing around her space. They wrapped her head in bandages, pulled bottles off the cabinets, and shoved pills into her mouth, forcing her to choke them down dry.

They hooked her up to a funny-looking machine. The machine was like an IV, but where the IV bag should have been was a dingy, rusty box with numbers scrawled on it. One of the faceless, protected doctors sat next to her and wheeled over a computer.

"Okay, Ayla, just a few more minutes. Then we'll get you fully decontaminated." The doctor's voice sounded like it was being filtered through machinery.

"H-How do you know my name?" The pain in her head let up enough to let her squeak out a few words.

The doctor looked at her and gave a muffled, robotic-sounding laugh. "You told us. Don't you remember?"

The pain in her head came back, and Ayla gritted her teeth. She let the feeling dwindle before speaking again. "I don't . . . remember much." She looked around again and stared at the IV-like tube in her arm. "Where am I?"

"You're in a hospital."

She gritted her teeth and clung to the bedsheets as the pain in her head flared up again.

"We have to decontaminate you, Ayla," the faceless voice said.

The pain passed, and Ayla opened her eyes. "Why?" she whispered.

"Because you came from the outside world. We can't have you infecting us."

Ayla was more confused than before and started to think that maybe she really was dead. She understood the concept of being decontaminated, and the fear people might have about contagions, but she came from a few stories above, not an alien planet.

"We haven't had to do this in quite a while. In fact, I don't think I've ever seen it used. What do you feel?"

Ayla didn't know how to respond. She shrugged. "My head hurts."

"What about other pain? Anything else besides the head? You can point to something if it's too painful to talk."

Ayla shook her head. Even if she had pain elsewhere, she couldn't identify it. The pulsing in her skull was distracting enough to take her mind off anything else.

"Your headache should go away eventually. What were you thinking, putting your head over an experiment like that?"

Ayla remembered that ball in the corner and the zapping sound, but the rest of her memories were fuzzy.

Something made a noise from the doctor's computer. The door in the front of the room opened, and two more people in protective suits came in. The doctor stood up and went over to them. They spoke, but their voices were muffled. Ayla strained to hear and quickly gave up after another rush of pain surged through her head.

She sank back into her bed and held on through the pain. After two more short but painful headaches came and went, the two new people came over and started wheeling her bed toward the door. The doctor came up to Ayla's side.

"Okay, Ayla, we have to take you to the decontamination room. I'm told it's a short procedure."

Ayla sighed and sank into her bed. She was at the mercy of these strangers—too weak to move and captured in an unfamiliar place.

The doctor patted Ayla's shoulder. "I'll see you there."

The two hazmat suits wheeled Ayla's bed through a series of confusing hallways. She paid no attention to the activity around her, except on the occasions when they passed a bright overhead light, when she would throw her hands over her face until they were past it.

For a hospital, however, there weren't as many bright lights as she expected, and some of the longer stretches of hallways had little to no light at all. They finally came to a room and stopped, then raised Ayla's bed into a sitting position. As she sat up, another hazmat suit walked into the room. The suit spoke in a familiar tone.

"Ayla, you're probably not going to like this, but I need you to stay calm and don't forget to breathe. Do you understand?"

Ayla's heart raced again. "What do you mean?"

The two hazmat suits next to her bed reached underneath Ayla's arms and started tying them to the bedside railings.

With a sudden jolt of energy, Ayla flailed her arms and kicked her feet. She let out a scream, but it sent a sharp pain into the back of her eyeballs. She ignored the blinding agony, trying anything to keep her hopes alive.

"Ayla," the familiar doctor shouted above the noise. "We need you to cooperate. Do you understand?"

Ayla kept kicking her legs and got in one good shot to one of the suits, but the suit quickly bounced back and clasped the arm restraint down tighter before moving onto her leg.

"Just remember to breathe," the doctor said.

Both her arms were tied up, and she shook the bed back and forth, trying to sway and rock and escape from the straps.

"This might feel weird, but it's for everyone's benefit, including your own, okay?"

Her last leg restraint locked into place and the two enforcers stepped back. She tried to kick again, but her legs didn't budge.

"Help me! H-Help!" Ayla yelled, hoping to either get help or wake up from this nightmare.

"Ayla, don't forget to breathe," the familiar doctor said.

A whirring sound kicked into gear as her bed dropped into the ground. Ayla strained her neck and head to look around the room. The doctor had taken a few steps back and now stood by the two other suits.

"What's happening?" Below her feet, above her head, and next to her sides, a glass panel rose out of the floor.

She was slowly being enclosed in a glass box.

Ayla fought the straps keeping her down. She continued gritting through the pain slamming into her head, rocking back and forth, trying to wriggle out. She screamed again.

The doctor and the suits didn't move from their spot in the

doorframe. They stood, their covered, emotionless faces watching her struggle and scream. Ayla tried kicking her feet and flexing her arms. The edges of the leather straps rubbed against her skin and burned her arms. The straps grew tighter, and she couldn't move at all. The top of the box closed in around her, and the glass dampened her weak screams. She stopped screaming and wriggling, finding it of no use. She watched the observers standing outside the glass box. The whirring sound stopped with a *click*. Ayla's heart thumped against her chest.

A dim light glowed from the box, as if the glass itself produced it. The light grew brighter and brighter until it forced Ayla to close her eyes. She kept squeezing them tighter until the light vanished completely. When she opened her eyes, she was engulfed by an eerie, inky-black nothingness.

The dim light rose again, and from somewhere below, a gurgling noise rose up, like water trying to run through a clogged drain. A lukewarm liquid crawled past her legs and against her back and neck. It felt oddly familiar, like the strawberry jelly goo she walked through before, and it had the same plastic smell. The puddle grew bigger and started filling the box.

Ayla screamed again, continuing to ignore the pain in her head. The puddle crept up her sides and legs and invaded her hair. It rose at an agonizingly slow pace, like syrup through a hose.

She scratched the bottom of the box with her fingertips and called out for help again, but she knew it wouldn't help.

The liquid filled Ayla's ears, and her screams reverberated in her head and added to the pain. The liquid continued to rise and covered the rest of her body.

She took a deep breath as the liquid approached her lips and nose.

She feared it might be her last breath ever.

The purple liquid crept over her lips, into her nose, and covered her eyes.

THREE

Captive Audience

Ayla woke up in a dark room. A blurry group of doctors loomed above her, looking down at her lying on another sterile hospital bed. Ayla's brain told her to run, but her body wouldn't cooperate. Instead, it flinched and startled the doctors overhead.

"Fascinating," a raspy voice said. "I'm surprised it worked."

"Why wouldn't it work?" A woman's voice this time.

Ayla tried to scream, but her mouth was numb and her muscles wouldn't move.

"Sorry about that. A nasty side effect. You'll be numb for another couple of hours." The voice sounded like the doctor from earlier, without the robotic-sounding voice. "There's not much we can do about it, but are you comfortable? You should be able to nod."

Ayla's body shook and her face was as hot as the middle of a bonfire. Her experience was anything but comfortable, so she swayed her head side to side.

The woman doctor laughed. "Comfortable is probably the wrong word. We have to monitor you for a while, okay?"

It was not okay, but Ayla wasn't in a position to negotiate.

"You're still in the hospital," the doctor said. "And we all have lots of questions for you when you're feeling up to it."

We all?

Ayla looked around but her vision was fuzzy. Two blurry people stood above her, and she was pretty sure she was no longer in the glass case. The woman doctor leaned in, and her face became clearer. "We'll be right back." Her skin was shockingly pale, and her washed-out lips formed a half-hearted smile. She patted Ayla's arm, then left the room with her colleague.

Ayla twitched again and wanted nothing more than to scream, to stand up and fight back, to do anything except lie in the bed. Sweat dripped from her forehead, and a tear formed in the corner of her eye.

Trapped again.

She had almost died at their hands, and now she couldn't even protect herself. She should have brought Derek, and she teared up at the thought of never seeing him again.

Why didn't I listen?

It was an adventure, but she wasn't sure it was what she wanted. The unknown wasn't nearly as comfortable as the life she had left behind. She wondered what she had gotten herself into.

Her eyes watered, and she blinked. She missed Derek. She missed her brother. She missed her mom. She had always missed her father, but even more so now, knowing she couldn't count on Dad to be her hero. She was disoriented and confused and missed the familiar feeling of closeness, the feeling of familiarity

44

she thought she didn't need. The coolness of the tears streaming down her cheeks relieved the burning in her face. She blinked them away and focused on the present.

What kind of hospital is this?

Ayla had no concept of the time that had passed since she left the apartment, but she hoped Derek was awake now, trying to find her. At a very minimum, she clung to the fact that he *was* back up above. Maybe his instincts would lead him to the building and he'd stumble upon her gloves and crowbar by the door she had told him about.

He could figure it out.

He *had* to figure it out.

Time dragged on, and Ayla wasn't sure if she'd move again. She had nothing to do but roll her eyes and head and check out the room imprisoning her. There were a few scattered chairs, and wires came out of the walls and ceiling. Along the far wall were glass cabinets with bottles of all shapes and sizes, and Ayla had to squint to make them out.

The dim light in the room came from colorful, glowing squares spaced randomly on all the walls. They looked like they were made of gel, maybe even the same purple goo she had almost drowned in. The blue ones looked like waves and the green ones grew brighter with each minute, then dimmed almost to black. The yellow squares didn't do much, and the orange ones pulsated every now and then.

After counting forty gel squares, Ayla was able to twitch some muscles in her legs. She didn't think it had been the couple of hours the doctor had predicted, but she was more than okay with a faster recovery.

At first, she wiggled her toes, then her fingers. After playing with the newfound sensation of movement again, she picked her knees up and bent her legs. A large smile ran across her face as she flexed her muscles. She stretched her arms across her body and scratched her head. She sat up in the bed and faced the wall of glowing orange squares, blinking a few times and letting her light-headedness pass.

Her unflattering, ill-fitting white hospital gown hung loosely off her body, exposing red marks and bruises on her wrists from the restraints, which were now gone. To try and ease the pain, she rubbed them softly. She closed her eyes for a moment and opened them again, confirming she wasn't dreaming, as the bright orange squares stayed stuck on the wall in front of her.

She felt more confident in her body, trusting her muscles to hold up their end of the bargain, so she swung her legs over the bed and plopped her bare feet on the floor. The concrete was cold, but the sensation was dull as her nerves tried to keep up. Ayla flexed her legs. It was like they had been asleep, tingling and painful. She pushed off the edge of the bed and stood, like a toddler struggling to find their center of gravity.

Getting used to controlling her own body again, she shifted her weight. The tingling in her legs eventually subsided and her strength started to return. To practice keeping balanced and moving her limbs, she swung her arms around.

The room was empty.

She was alone.

This is my chance.

Ayla didn't want to suffer alone in a strange, unfamiliar hospital with doctors hovering around her. She pictured her mom lying in hospice, waiting to die. Ayla was lucky enough to have the opportunity to change something about her situation, a luxury her mom was never afforded.

She moved from one foot to the other, double-checking her balance and strength with every step. She got close to a wall of multicolored gel squares and reached out to stabilize herself. Her fingers grazed the edge of a couple of green and orange squares and started to sink in, almost like she had put her hand in quicksand.

She jerked them back out, not knowing the consequences for leaving her hand in there, and readjusted her positioning, placing her hand on a small space between some colored cells. As she shuffled along the wall, her hand grazed free space until she was within striking distance of the door. Her legs hurt and she felt cold and short of breath, but she had to keep going.

She had to reach the door.

She had to escape.

Ayla balanced against the wall and tried to shake out the soreness of her arms and legs. Her balance improved, but her nerves betrayed her and stung in all the wrong places. She grasped her calf muscles and tried to massage out the strain.

She eyed the door and guessed it would take no more than ten steps to reach it. Sighing heavily, she let go of the wall and took a large step forward. As her foot landed hard against the concrete, a clicking sound came from the door, which inched open.

Panic raced through her mind, and she paused mid-step. Her heart raced and the thumping of the blood rushing through her head sounded louder than ever. She wasn't sure what to expect when the door opened, but she didn't have the time or energy to scramble back to her bed and pretend like nothing had happened.

Ayla looked around, trying to find something to grab if she had to defend herself, but there was nothing within reach. The door continued to creep open while she stood and watched.

"Ayla?" a voice came from behind the door. Ayla didn't respond and instead stood there, staring. The door opened a bit more, and a face appeared. "Ayla?" The woman doctor from before slowly nudged the door open with her shoulder, gazed around the room, and made eye contact with Ayla. "What are you doing over there?"

The doctor jogged over to the bed and grabbed the top blanket, then headed back for Ayla, who flinched and tried to throw her hands up in defense but found her muscles weak from the jaunt across the room. The doctor threw the blanket around Ayla's shoulders and squeezed them lightly. "You must be exhausted." The doctor guided Ayla back to the bed. "Sit down and let me get you something to eat."

Ayla was silent, sitting on the bed, wrapped in a blanket, not sure how to react to this doctor who acted like her mother when hours ago she thought she was trying to kill her.

The doctor went over to one of the walls and opened a small cabinet door, where she pressed a few buttons before the door closed again.

"I hope you like soup," she said as she came back to the bed to sit down next to Ayla. "What were you doing over there?" She placed the steaming bowl of soup on a tray next to Ayla's bed.

Ayla leaned away from the stranger, avoiding eye contact, staring into her soup bowl. The yellow liquid smelled like warm chicken broth and reminded her of home. It would be nice to eat, but she was suspicious.

"You know what? I've been rude. I'm sorry." The doctor cleared her throat and stuck out her hand. "I'm Katherine. It's nice to officially meet you."

Ayla raised her hand and then paused and searched Katherine's face before extending her own hand as much as she could.

Katherine grasped it like an egg. "You're freezing," she said. "Here, take this."

She cupped Ayla's hands with one of her own. Ayla tried to pull back, but Katherine was insistent. She grabbed the soup bowl with her free hand and placed it in Ayla's.

Once Ayla was comfortable with the weight, she reached for a spoon on the tray and shoveled the warm broth into her mouth, not remembering the last meal she had.

"And, Ayla," the doctor said as Ayla consumed another spoonful of warm liquid, "we'll have to restrain you to the bed this time." Katherine patted her leg. "We can't have you trying to escape."

"Ayla, I need to understand why you're here. Can you tell me why you're here?"

Ayla was bound to her hospital bed by wrist and leg restraints now, sitting and propped up against the raised bed to be face to face with Katherine, her interviewer. The restraints held her bound to whatever schedule the doctors prescribed for her.

Soup meals came and went, causing a roller coaster in Ayla's gut that matched the roller coaster ride in her mind as she tried to sort everything out. She assumed she was still underground, but every question she asked was met with either silence or more questions. She had been told very little so far.

Ayla played back the facts as she knew them: she was in a hospital, and she had been decontaminated because they saw her as a threat from the "outside world," whatever that meant. Anything beyond that was speculation on her part. She had tried not to reveal any more information than was absolutely necessary, to the doctors or to the nurses, but it was starting to become a challenge, and now Katherine sat in front of her, pen and paper pad in hand, sitting cross-legged in an uncomfortable-looking hard plastic chair. In the bright lights of the room, Katherine's skin was paler than Ayla had remembered. She looked like a skeleton with a ponytail. Katherine stared wide-eyed at Ayla, who now remembered that she had been asked a question.

"I stumbled onto what looked like a door and . . . I just got curious."

"How, specifically, did you 'stumble' here?" Katherine put air quotes over the word "stumble," and for the first time, Ayla saw how skinny her fingers were.

"It's important that you don't leave out any details." Katherine used her skinny fingers to scribble wildly on her pad of paper.

"I stumbled on this old"— Ayla fumbled to come up with the right word but finally landed on one—"disc in the ground, in an abandoned building when I was exploring an area of the city."

"Are all of the buildings abandoned?" Katherine pointed her pencil at the ceiling. "Up there? In the city?"

Ayla assumed that was confirmation that she was underground, and although she was confused, she continued to humor Katherine. "No."

"What else is up there?" Katherine asked without looking up from her paper.

Ayla was still confused, a common theme. She stuck to her

initial plan of not giving out more information than she had to. "What do you mean?"

"I mean, where you came from, what's it like?"

"It's okay, I guess." While not true, given Ayla's recent experiences, it was the only *safe* answer she could think to give. "Normal," she said. Thrown off by the direction of their conversation, she didn't know what else to say. She tried to change the focus. "What's it like down here?"

Katherine ignored her question. "Ayla, you have to be truthful or I can't help you." She tapped her pencil on her pad of paper as she talked. "Who are you working for?"

Ayla paused, having difficulties finding a response to the odd question. Katherine stared back at her, and the two locked eyes for an uncomfortably long period of time, and the words were practically squeezed out of Ayla's throat. "I have two jobs. I work in a restaurant and a bar. Katherine, I don't know what you want me to say."

"Why are you here?" Katherine pressed.

Thoughts and words swirled around in Ayla's head. She searched for the right ones to pluck out of the air to meet Katherine's satisfaction, but she couldn't find any. The questions didn't make sense, and she wasn't sure correct answers existed. She felt like the kid in class who wasn't listening to the teacher but was called on to answer. Her face went flush, and she blurted out the next best thing she could think of. "I don't know!"

"Tell me the truth."

"I already told you the truth."

"Nobody stumbles on this place, Ayla. I know about life above ground, so just tell me the truth."

KEVIN MORAN

"I *am* telling you the truth. I live in an apartment, have a couple shitty jobs, and explore things for fun." Tears tugged at Ayla's eyelids again, and she tried to suppress them. "I don't know what else you want me to say, honestly." She sniffled and tried to wipe her nose against her shoulder.

"Listen, Ayla, you're a threat to us down here. If you don't stop lying to me, I won't be able to help you escape whatever punishment comes your way."

Ayla's vision tunneled in on Katherine's face. The words "threat" and "punishment" stuck in her brain.

What is Katherine talking about? Where the hell am I?

"I don't know what's going on, okay? But I'm pretty sure I'm not who you think I am."

"Are you a threat?"

"No!" Ayla shook her head. She couldn't believe what she was hearing. "Why would I be a threat? How in the world am I a threat to anybody?" Growing up, Ayla and her family always got suspicious glances and sideways looks in their small town, and now, she had the same feelings all over again. She was an outsider—and a threat.

"This place has been around since the late nineteenth century. In those one-hundred-plus years, we've had no contact with anyone like you from the outside world," Katherine said. "Why, suddenly, have you shown up? I find your story *very* difficult to believe. You simply *stumbled* on something that nobody else has in over a century?"

"Look, I don't know anything about this place other than what you've told me. I have no interest in threatening anyone. I just want to go home."

52

Katherine sighed and looked down at her notes. She flipped the paper back over and reread everything on the prior pages. Ayla hoped she had given her what she needed, at least for now. She had to formulate another plan to escape. If she was seen as a threat, she knew that, eventually, she'd be forced out, one way or another.

Katherine sighed again and looked up. "What building were you in when you found that . . . disc, I think you called it?"

"An old warehouse. It's been abandoned for as long as I can remember."

Katherine scratched out more notes. "Can you describe this disc in more detail?"

Ayla reached back into her memory. "It was round and pretty small. A few circles inside, and the word 'Aura' was engraved in the middle. My boyfriend didn't think it was a big deal . . ." Ayla immediately regretted what she'd said. Heat spread throughout her face as she watched Katherine stop writing and look up from her paper.

"Your boyfriend?" Katherine asked. "Someone else was with you?"

"He was just there once," Ayla blurted. She pulled at her restraints, trying to physically grab her words out of the air and take them back. "He doesn't know how to get down here. He saw the marker in the building. That's all. He wanted to go back to the apartment because he thought it wasn't safe."

Katherine scribbled and, without saying a word, stood up, kicked her chair back, and walked for the door.

"Katherine, I promise he doesn't know anything." Ayla leaned against her restraints again. "Katherine!"

Katherine reached the door and turned around. "I'll be right back." With the ominous statement, the door slammed shut, and Ayla found herself alone again with her thoughts and regret.

Her chin dropped to her chest. The front of her shirt was wet from tears. She let it slip that a second party knew about the entrance to this place, and she had no idea how dangerous that was.

Did I just put Derek's life in danger?

She wasn't sure where Derek was or if he was coming after her. Hopefully he was kicking down and busting through doors, acting the hero role to come and save her. She hoped he didn't wind up suffering a similar fate.

The thought caused more tears to well up and roll onto the front of her shirt, but she didn't care anymore. She was locked away in a mysterious hospital with weird procedures, getting probed with questions she didn't understand by people she couldn't trust.

Who is Katherine?

She stopped to think about what she really knew about her. Ayla didn't like the word "captor" but wasn't sure what else made sense. Katherine seemed to care for Ayla's well-being, bringing her food, wrapping her in a blanket, always making sure to ask how she was and doing her best to make her comfortable.

But Katherine was also responsible for having her restrained and for asking judgmental questions as if she didn't trust her. Katherine also put her in the decontamination goo that had almost killed her.

What am I doing?

All Ayla had been looking for was some adventure, some way to spice up her life and lift her out of her funk. Until recently, she never really knew what depression was like. It was like she was in a hole she couldn't climb out of. She could see the top, she could see the light and how great it was outside of the hole, but no matter how hard she tried, or how hard she wanted to not be in the hole, she couldn't make it to the top. It was aggravating, and now, as she sat here, restrained to a bed, those feelings washed over her again.

Ayla sighed.

The door clicked open, and Katherine walked back in.

"Katherine." Ayla perked up and turned as best as she could to face Katherine. "Look, I—"

"Don't worry, Ayla." Katherine's long stride carried her to the chair she had left next to Ayla's bed, and she took a seat with her notebook in her lap. She dropped her pencil on top and looked at Ayla, staring forward with her mouth shut. "I don't want you to think poorly of me." Katherine looked around and held her hands out. "Of *us*."

An ominous feeling punched Ayla in the gut.

"But I do want you to know we're cautious and guarded, especially given the circumstances of how you ended up here."

"I understand, but—" Ayla tried to interject again.

"I can protect you if I know the truth, but know that if I can't get a straight answer from you, your life is in jeopardy. I'll have to turn you over to our security forces, and they won't be as nice as I am."

"But I *am* telling you the truth!"

"It's not good enough!" Katherine yelled back.

"What do you want, Katherine?"

"Just an answer. I *want* to protect you, Ayla. I can help you get out of here if you just listen to me."

"How can I trust you?"

"I'm the only one you have, okay? You can either trust me or you can continue fighting an unwinnable battle. It's your choice, but it doesn't seem like much of a choice to me."

Ayla swallowed the lump in her throat and dropped her head back into the pillow. She wanted to bust out of her restraints and wring Katherine's skinny neck, shake her until she knew the full story, and then run off and never return. She wanted to change things but sighed instead.

Katherine opened her notebook and flipped to the last page.

"So, your boyfriend, what's his name anyway?"

Ayla hesitantly replied with a weak-sounding "Derek." She had already given him up; she might as well try to build some level of trust with Katherine. Her choices seemed limited, but that didn't mean she couldn't try to work them to her favor.

"And you said he saw the disc with you?"

"Yes, in the abandoned building."

"And what was so special about this disc?" Katherine pressed.

"Well, there were three rings on the inside, with the word 'Aura' engraved inside of a five-point star."

Katherine scribbled away at her notepad as Ayla kept talking.

"And when I pulled at the rings, the floor started coming away from the ground, like an old trapdoor."

"Interesting . . ." Katherine's voice faded, and her eyes stayed glued to her notepad.

"And then there was this old ladder that led to a hallway—" Ayla paused mid-sentence. She wasn't sure why it hadn't crossed her mind before. "My camera," she blurted out.

Katherine looked up in surprise. "Your camera?"

"My camera. It's in my bag. I had it with me. Where's my backpack?" She sat up and looked around.

"Why?"

"I can show you exactly what it looked like. I took all sorts of pictures of that place. If you can give me my camera, I can show you." Ayla's eyes widened and her hope returned.

If there was any way to prove to Katherine that she was telling the truth, she imagined photographic evidence would be the easiest. Katherine would have to believe her. Ayla hoped her camera had survived the trip and was hanging around somewhere in one piece.

"Okay," Katherine said.

Ayla relaxed back into her pillow. "I promise, Katherine, that this will help clear everything up. I can show you the building, the city, my apartment, our—"

"I can check on it this afternoon. How's that?" Katherine interrupted with a smile.

"The sooner, the better."

"Great." Katherine stuck her nose back into her notebook and jotted down a few notes before moving on to more questions. "You said you worked in a restaurant. Can you tell me more about that?"

Ayla had changed her mind about giving Katherine more information. Her goal was now to build as much trust as possible, get on her good side, and at least have one ally here. She rattled off details about her boss, her coworkers, and her latest shift while trying to keep up with all of Katherine's questions, which seemed to bounce between relevant topics and things that didn't seem to matter much. It was mentally exhausting.

The only other thing keeping Ayla going was the hope that

somewhere her camera was out there, offering some type of proof that could help set her free. After Ayla ran through what seemed like her whole life story, Katherine was out of free space in her notebook and only had one question left.

"What would you like for dinner?"

FOUR

Following Protocol

"I'm not sure what to think, Jeffrey." Katherine walked over to the bookshelf in the corner of her dingy office. She was one of the lucky few to have the light of a small desk lamp and a dim overhead bulb. Her hand found the top shelf, moved past her old, dusty biology textbooks from the turn of the century, and found its way to the more recently put-together loose-leaf paper binder.

"I'm not sure you'll find anything there," Jeffrey said from the opposite corner of the room. He sat on a couch-like surface comprised of old packing material and cardboard. Jeffrey reached up and moved his glasses back from the end of his long nose to their rightful home between his eyes. "This is a fairly unusual circumstance."

"We followed the protocol, right?"

Jeffrey bobbed his head. "Absolutely."

Katherine flipped the loose-leaf binder open, exposing the middle of the book. "And according to page 314 of the protocol guide, we're supposed to run tests and turn the subject over to security detail." She pointed to the passage as she walked over to Jeffrey, who sat on the couch.

"That is what the protocol says, yes," Jeffrey answered. He took a puff from his cigarette and let it hang between his fingers.

"I don't know if I can hand her over to Clay." She locked eyes with Jeffrey. "She does *not* seem dangerous."

"Assuming she was sent here to gather secrets and steal technology, isn't that what she would want you to think?"

"I think I'm a good judge of character," Katherine said. Jeffrey nodded in agreement. "And I don't sense anything from her that's concerning. She seems genuinely scared and unaware of anything down here."

Jeffrey shrugged. "Maybe she's a really good actor."

"Anything is possible, I guess . . ." Katherine trailed off and stared at page 314 again to make sure she had read it right. "What if the protocol is wrong?"

"It's not wrong, Katherine."

"What if it *is* wrong?"

"It's not," Jeffrey insisted.

"You're not listening to me."

"No, I am listening. I just know it's not wrong." Jeffrey brushed his thick, graying mustache and stuck his cigarette into his mouth. He took another slow drag. "Why do you think protocol is wrong?"

Katherine sat in a lopsided rolling chair across from the couch. She dropped the protocol papers, propped open to page 314, in her lap and let her elbows rest on them.

"I can't describe it. I just have a feeling. It's my instinct."

Jeffrey sighed, sending a plume of smoke through the room.

"We're doctors. We're not here to make decisions based on our 'gut feelings,' Katherine." Jeffrey's long fingers provided air quotes. "We are here to follow proper guidelines to ensure safety and security of our patients and subjects."

"But I don't think it's a matter of safety *or* security."

"It's pure security," Jeffrey said. "How do you think she got in here? Her explanation of 'stumbling' in won't get much support outside of her own head. You know she won't get sympathy from Clay."

Katherine leaned back in the wobbly chair and ran her fingers through her hair. "I know," she said. "But I think she deserves the benefit of the doubt."

"Why?" Jeffrey glanced in Katherine's direction. "I see two possibilities. In one instance, she's a spy attempting to undermine us. In the other, she's a complete liar."

"That's pretty narrow-minded," Katherine said.

"Do you even remember the last time Clay had to be involved?"

"This is different," Katherine insisted.

"It's not that different," Jeffrey said. "A small faction of people here planned an uprising and were actively trying to escape. They were almost acting like internal spies, in a way. Once the rumors got out, Clay stepped in and squashed it immediately. Just be thankful you were on the right side that time." He sat up in the makeshift couch. "Don't be on the wrong side this time. Don't be like your predecessor . . ."

Katherine sighed. "I know."

"I'm just telling you," Jeffrey continued. "Don't forget there's still a war going on above us. We're here for a reason, Katherine. We're here to protect our side and support the war effort. The minute you or others start thinking about not backing the effort one hundred percent . . ." Instead of finishing his thought, Jeffrey took a drag from his ever-dwindling cigarette.

"I get your point, Jeffrey," Katherine said. "I just need more time to find the full truth."

Jeffrey interjected. "You may not have the luxury of time."

"I need to keep building trust with her. I think we're in a good spot. I just don't know what else to do." Katherine stared down at the loose-leaf binder in her lap. She picked it up and flipped through it again, not knowing what she was looking for.

Jeffrey slouched on the couch, close to finishing his cigarette, and stared off into space.

"Why are you so negative? Why can't you trust her?" Katherine said out of the blue.

"Why are you so easily trusting?" Jeffrey sat up, his cigarette dangling from the edge of his mouth. "I have a different perspective. That's all. In this case, I think it's good. In fact, I think I should talk to her."

"Why?" Katherine looked at him sideways.

"Different perspective," Jeffrey said with a smile.

Katherine bit her lip. She had worked with Jeffrey for a long time, and she recalled how long it took for her to fully trust him. Now, with Ayla's life on the line, all her doubts from the beginning flooded back. He did make sense though, and another opinion might help shed light on the issue. Protocol didn't say anything about it, and in the end, she valued Jeffrey's opinion more than anyone else's. "Are you free this afternoon?" she asked.

"I have some patients I need to attend to, but I should have some availability in a few hours."

"I'll stop by, and we can head over. Does that work?" Katherine stood up.

"Sure," Jeffrey said, stamping out his cigarette.

"I will swing by then. And, Jeffrey," she continued, "I'd appreciate you picking up your trash." She pointed at his cigarette, which Jeffrey had casually discarded on the cockeyed table.

Katherine stepped out from the hospital entrance and into the central hub of town, known as the central square. At this time of day, this part of town was packed full of merchants, vendors, and people milling about. She paused and gazed upward, past the three stories of only partially full rooms and offices, and stared at the fixture hanging above.

It was oval-shaped and looked like an enormous semitransparent sliver of glass. Breathing in the fresh air it provided, she took a second to reflect on the accomplishments of her colleagues. She opened her palms to soak in the sunrays beaming through the one-way portal above her.

She was grateful they had this giant portal—what people referred to as *the Mirror*—instead of the dingy, empty, and dreary atmosphere they lived in before. Before the Mirror was installed, she had seen her fair share of dietary changes and vitamin D supplements. It wasn't even that long ago, but life had changed drastically since then.

The other focal point of the central square was *the Beacon*, a large round building spiraling up toward the ceiling in the middle of the square. It was a fancy soapbox the leaders used for announcements.

Katherine had primarily seen it used by research and

development to underscore recent findings or tell the world of its latest discovery. She wasn't sure if it was in use anymore, as the last time she remembered any announcement coming from the Beacon was the day she first heard about portals.

When they installed the Mirror was when she first realized the true potential of the portals. Not only could people move from one place to another faster and easier, but the portals had the potential to significantly change the way people lived their lives.

She bobbed and weaved her way through crowds, every so often stepping off the main marble path and onto the dirt floor or surrounding wooden supports. With clean clothes that fit right and a face free of dirt smears, she stood out among the crowd. Everyone knew her, as she had seen them all come through the hospital at least once, and she was used to the stares and so just smiled and kept on her way.

Katherine loathed what the central square had become. Instead of a forum for open civic debates and discussions on the latest philosophical ideas, it had turned into a haphazard marketplace littered with makeshift kiosks and pop-up tents where the less-fortunate people of the facility scrimped and scraped everything they had to buy supplies, clothing, food, or whatever luxury they could afford that month. Katherine was one of the few who lived above the central square, and she was thankful every day for her good fortune and position.

Katherine normally didn't stop on her strolls through the central square, but the wafting smell of freshly roasted coffee caught her attention, and she paused in front of a makeshift coffee shop and approached the register. This coffee kiosk, like most in the central square, was a temporary building in the loosest sense of the word. It was a battered tent propped up by stakes driven into the soft parts of the ground or hammered into the parts of the floor that had been covered by wood.

"What can I get you?" The man behind the old, clunky register coughed into his long, ill-fitting sleeve. His outfit was full of holes and patches from previous cover-up work. He wiped dirt from his forehead, and his greasy hair slid to the side.

"Just one coffee, please," Katherine said. She started to dig in her pocket for payment. The man punched a few numbers with loud clunks into the register. Katherine hovered her hand above his and dropped the money into his bandaged palm.

"Thank you," his rough voice said. "Give me one minute." The coins clanked against the register as he tossed them in before heading inside the tent.

Katherine knew coffee was more of a luxury item here, compared to other things. She wasn't sure how Jeffrey acquired all of his tobacco, but she assumed he knew a guy who could help him out. It was easier for Katherine and Jeffrey and others in positions of power to obtain what they needed.

The supplies were all carefully managed by a team down in the lower levels below the central square. The people in town were more or less born into their roles, but as technology advanced, many found themselves without a purpose and turned to peddling supplies and goods in the central square. The man serving her coffee was from infrastructure, she was pretty sure.

The man returned, this time with a small cup of coffee in his non-bandaged hand. "Thank you, ma'am," he said, handing the coffee over to Katherine.

As she reached out for the cup, she dropped another coin onto his counter. "That's just for you," she said.

The man's eyes lit up, and he quickly picked up the coin and put it into his own pocket. "Thank you!" he said.

Katherine smiled and turned back toward the main path. She hung her head and stuck her nose near her coffee. She felt bad, and empathy was something she had to work on. She was too sympathetic to everyone in the facility, and she knew the situation wasn't going to improve for most. Maybe the same was holding her back from truly evaluating and understanding Ayla.

Am I being too sympathetic with her?

She was especially glad now that she had decided to let Jeffrey talk to Ayla, to make sure there were multiple inputs going forward. With such a big decision on the line and with them moving into new, uncharted territory, she was coming around to the idea of getting even more feedback. She was hoping Mr. Fixer had good news for her too.

The short walk to the other side of the central square didn't take long, but she was able to finish her small coffee and toss it into one of the overflowing trash bins off the main path. It was sometimes hard to know what was trash and what wasn't with so many garbage-looking tents and buildings and pieces of furniture and actual trash littering the pathways. Katherine tried her best to respect the rules and keep her corner of the world in control.

At a large elevator door, she pushed the button off to the side of the wall and waited. She never liked heading to the lower levels, as it wasn't her place to be, so she tried to avoid it at all costs; the looks became weirder as she went farther down. When the elevator doors dinged and opened, she stepped inside and pushed the M button.

People called him "Mr. Fixer," but nobody was quite sure how the name came to be. Katherine stood an arm's length away from his workbench and watched as he fiddled furiously with wires and strings and goo. The dexterity in his fingers allowed him to pick up small, barely visible pieces in the midst of his fast motions.

Sweat dripped down his chest, darkening his red shirt, and his brown overalls seemed to have more holes than not. The pool of sweat grew on his chest and made his head shine in the reflection of the halogen lights hanging by chains above his workbench. She realized that people must have seen him work, and the nickname stuck.

Though Katherine hated coming down to the lower levels and tried to avoid it, on a few occasions, she had to make a few compromises. The last time she was here was to drop off Ayla's backpack, which had been tossed aside, the contents spilling out onto the workbench.

"Welcome back," the bald man said from behind his bench. His deep voice startled Katherine, even though she expected it. He didn't look up, and his arms continued moving around the table, working diligently on things in front of him.

"I just wanted to check in and see if you've come across anything new worth mentioning."

Mr. Fixer paused his frantic work and looked up. "Nothing major."

Katherine took one step forward. "What all was in her backpack?"

"You might be interested in a couple things." He opened the front pouch on the backpack, grabbed a wallet, and tossed it to Katherine, who tried to grab it out of the air but missed.

After picking it up off the floor, she ruffled around inside, undoing zippers and shuffling things around. "An ID card," she said. Mr. Fixer didn't turn his attention away from his workbench. "Issued in 2008 . . ." She flipped the card over and inspected it. "Do you know what this means?" She directed the question at Mr. Fixer, but he still didn't look up. "There *is* a recent form of a city up there, not just a war-torn wasteland. Maybe she isn't lying."

"Those can be faked." Mr. Fixer's voice boomed from behind his workbench. "Besides, that's not all." He reached down and opened a drawer. He pulled out Ayla's camera and plopped it on the table.

Katherine approached the table and snatched the camera. "Do you know how to work it?"

"Kind of. But the power is running low, and I haven't figured out how to get juice to it yet." He pointed to a blue, glowing bowl of gel on his desk. "Our boosters don't seem to want to work with it."

"But it still works?" Katherine fiddled with the buttons.

"As far as I can tell . . ."

"What else do you have there?"

Mr. Fixer stopped moving and looked at Katherine. "That's what I'm trying to find out." He wiped sweat off his forehead, then scattered a few things around the table and left a black, rectangular piece of equipment sitting in the middle. Katherine didn't recognize any of the odd markings carved into it.

"This," Mr. Fixer said, picking up the mysterious rectangle, "is something I'm not familiar with. It looks like a thick keycard but doesn't work the same way. I did a few routine checks, mostly looking for explosives or incendiaries." He looked up at Katherine. "Standard safety checks. Nothing out of the ordinary. What's really bizarre," he continued, now searching his workbench for something, "is when I pull up a standard diagnostic run, I can see familiar-looking components, but I can't seem to access them."

He pulled out a slim screen attached to a bowl of green gel, like the square on the wall in Katherine's hospital. She had seen the gel—also known as boosters—used in a lot of different places here, but never quite like this before. Mr. Fixer dropped the item in the gel, and the screen attached to the bowl fired up and started spitting out numbers and symbols Katherine never had to worry about before. She left that up to technicians and people like Mr. Fixer.

"What's that telling you?" Katherine pointed to the screen with symbols she interpreted as belonging to a foreign language.

"It's telling me that I have to keep working, but I may need her help."

"Ayla's?" Katherine asked.

Mr. Fixer glanced up briefly and then focused his attention back on the rectangular object in the gel bowl.

For as long as she had known him, Mr. Fixer had *never* asked for help. "How much more time can you put into it?"

"It's my top priority, but Lee has me looking into this orb too." He pointed to the edge of his workbench, where a shiny blue ball sat. Katherine didn't recognize it, but that wasn't unusual, given where she was. "He said he needs it soon. I'm not sure how long that will take me."

"Keep working on Ayla's things. I can tell Lee it's more urgent than whatever he's got for you."

Mr. Fixer looked up at Katherine and wiped his face again with his forearm. "Can you give me any other information? Maybe something new from your talks with her?"

"I can send you a dump of my latest interview, but I don't think it'll be anything earth-shattering."

Mr. Fixer muttered under his breath and went back to work, leaning heavily against his wooden workbench. It was once painted red, but with so many chipped-off spots, it was nearly back to wood grain. "I'll keep an eye out for it. If anything changes, you know where to find me."

"Thank you." Katherine spun on her heel, anxious to leave this place and take the camera back to Ayla.

FIVE

Attempt to Leave

Ayla had nurses stop by from time to time, and today, the nurse was a plump older woman wearing blue scrubs and her hair up in a bun.

"Can I use the restroom?" Ayla asked.

"Sure. Let me just take care of this real quick," the nurse said, walking over to a monitor on a far wall. After pushing a few buttons, the nurse waddled to Ayla's bed, grabbed a card from her pocket, then held it up against the restraints. The restraints beeped and popped open. She held out her hand. "You ready?"

Ayla grabbed the nurse's arm, swung her feet over the bed, and stood up, careful to use the pudgy nurse as leverage to maintain her balance. Her knees wobbled and knocked together. She tightened her grip on the nurse as she adjusted to her position outside of the bed. Being bed-ridden was something Ayla wasn't used to, and she didn't realize her muscles would start weakening over time. It felt like she had been in bed for months.

71

"Thanks again," Ayla said, standing straighter and testing her muscles.

"That's what I'm here for." The nurse led Ayla to the restroom, on the opposite corner of the room, past all the glowing gel squares and panels that were familiar to Ayla now.

She had seen them used a few times—once when a nurse set a silver disc inside an orange one that pulled up a display of Ayla's vital stats, and another time when a keycard was put in, which then pulled up a blueprint of her room and the surrounding area.

It had been late at night, and the nurse must have assumed Ayla was asleep. Ayla stayed as quiet as the night she and Derek were chased by the armed guard and had opened her eyes just enough to take a mental picture of the screen. She saw a long hallway outside her room, with side doors, closets, and a large door at the end. Beyond the door was a large room labeled "central" something.

Ayla's less-than-photographic memory had failed her, and the nurse only had the screen up for a few seconds before she grabbed the keycard out of the orange goo. Ayla had spent the rest of that day drawing the map over and over in her head. If she ever had a chance to make a break for it, she assumed she'd need at least a vague idea of where she was going, because the last time she started running for freedom, she ended up surrounded by people and thrown into the hospital.

Ayla shuffled, hand in hand, with the nurse to the bathroom. The nurse opened the door and led Ayla in. A buzzing sound rang out from the nurse's pocket.

"I have to step outside real quick, okay?" the nurse said, reaching into her pocket to turn off whatever had made the sound.

"Was that the keycard?" Ayla asked, trying to peek into the nurse's pocket.

"Don't go anywhere, okay?" A large smile ran across the nurse's face. She backed away from the bathroom door and called out one last time. "Just yell for me if you need me . . ." Her voice trailed off as she disappeared down the hallway.

Ayla was left standing in the bathroom, alone, without supervision, without restraints for the first time that she could remember. It had been at least a couple of days, but for Ayla, it had felt like a couple of weeks. She hadn't planned anything, but without warning, her circumstances had changed. This was her chance. This was what she had been waiting for. It was now or never, so she pulled up her mental model of the map and scrambled to remember if there were any other doors or spots to run to.

Is there a janitorial closet in the hallway?

She cursed her less-than-perfect memory. Her map was incomplete, with huge gaps, and the only thing she remembered was the *central* room, and she hoped that room was either the way out or the way to find help. She scanned the bathroom for anything useful, but not knowing how much time she would have, she decided against taking anything.

Ayla slowly opened the bathroom door and stepped back out into the room, then tiptoed to the cracked-open entrance and peered outside. Her nurse had her back to the room, her keycard pinned against her ear like a phone. She was talking and distracted, so Ayla inched the door open enough to slip through. Her back against the wall, she carefully and methodically walked in the opposite direction down the hallway until she was out of sight of her nurse.

The map in her mind kept showing her the way—straight down the hallway to the central room. The nurse was still occupied, so Ayla half-walked and half-jogged down the hallway. She scooted past more hospital room doors, and the overhead halogen lights buzzed and reflected a bright white light off all the smooth, sterile surfaces. From top to bottom, the hallway glistened white, the sight blurring as Ayla broke into a run.

Her freedom waited at the end of the hallway.

She found herself sprinting now, her smooth-soled shoes not finding much grip on the floor.

Afraid of falling, she slowed down as she approached a large door. The overweight nurse had caught onto the fact that her patient had escaped, but she lagged behind farther down the hallway.

Ayla slammed into the door. It was labeled "Central Square." There was no handle, so Ayla searched for a way to open it. The nurse was closer, but still far enough away for Ayla to find an escape. She pounded her fists against the obstacle in front of her, then turned to the keycard scanner off to the right. She pushed buttons next to it, waved her hands in front of it, and tried everything she could think of to move the door.

The nurse was closing in. There was a buzzing noise, and the door started disappearing into the ceiling. When the door got high enough, Ayla ducked and darted through the low opening, running directly into a pair of legs. She dropped to the floor.

"Ayla?"

She tried to turn around and run the other way, but a hand reached out and grabbed her arm. Though she tried to fight off the grip, it stayed strong, seemingly without effort, and reached out and took hold of her other arm. Ayla stopped her escape efforts and turned to face her captor. It was a tall man, and Katherine stood next to him.

"Katherine," Ayla said, out of breath and in a not-quite-a-question but also not-quite-a-statement kind of way.

"I'm disappointed." Katherine sighed and motioned to the nurse down the hall. "This is going to make my job a lot harder, Ayla."

Ayla once again found herself bound to her bed.

Two large men dragged her back to her room, tightened the restraints, and added one more across her waist like a seat belt for good measure. She had a feeling she wasn't going to have too many more free-roaming bathroom breaks, and she probably wouldn't see that nurse again. Katherine and the man who had grabbed her in the hallway loomed over her bed.

"Ayla, this is my colleague Jeffrey."

"I'm so sorry we had to officially meet in such an unfortunate way, Ayla," Jeffrey said. The smell of cigarette smoke rolled out of his mouth. "Katherine has been so kind as to provide a copious amount of information about you so far. I feel like I know you quite well, actually."

He locked eyes with Ayla and waited for a response. When he didn't get one, he continued.

"I do have to say, however, that what my colleague has communicated to me about you, of course, has not been on the positive side but rather negative. Having said that, I still, and I believe Katherine still does as well, have a considerable number of questions for you."

"Katherine's already asked me a lot," Ayla blurted.

"Ayla," Katherine chimed in. "Jeffrey is here so that we can get a different perspective."

"I don't have anything different to say," Ayla replied.

"My aim is to gain an additional perspective on the situation," Jeffrey said. "We aren't the bad guys, Ayla."

Ayla tugged at her restraints. "A little hard to believe."

"I think we're getting off on the wrong foot . . ." Katherine reached into her pocket. "Here." She pulled out Ayla's camera and set it in Ayla's lap. "I got this from our technician earlier today."

"Does it still work?" Ayla asked, reaching for the camera as best as she could.

Jeffrey let out a *humph* sound and leaned in to snatch the camera.

"It's okay. He ran it through tests. It's safe." Katherine grabbed the camera from Jeffrey. "He said it's low on power, so we may not have a lot of time."

"Can you free my hands?" Ayla asked. "I can't show you anything unless I can work with it." She did her best puppy-dog expression.

Katherine and Jeffrey exchanged glances. "You can tell me what to do," Katherine said.

"Please, be very careful with it." Ayla looked at Katherine and waited for a nod before continuing. "There's a switch on top that turns it on."

Katherine turned the switch to the *on* position, and the camera came to life. A blue screen popped up and flashed the brand's logo before bringing the viewer into frame. Katherine waved the camera around, watching the room through the screen, and pointed it at Jeffrey. "This is much nicer than anything we have."

Ayla glanced at the power indicator. "We don't have a lot of time left. Can you come a little closer?" Katherine moved in closer and pointed the screen toward Ayla. "Now, press the button with the little triangle on it. It's near the bottom." Katherine searched for a minute before finding and pressing the button that brought Ayla's previous pictures to the screen. The first image was a fuzzy, grainy picture of the door underneath the abandoned building. "I think the images may be a bit corrupt," Ayla said, leaning in. "But this is the door I came in through. You see there?" Ayla pointed to the screen. "WW-8, on the door." She looked up at Katherine and Jeffrey, who now crowded around the screen. "Do you know what that is?"

"Eight!" Jeffrey proclaimed with fascination. "I didn't know an eight even existed."

"That's an old door," Katherine said. "We should run it by Ellen, right? She might know."

"Or that we have operating wall walkers anymore . . ." Jeffrey continued, ignoring Katherine's comments.

"Wall walker?" Ayla asked.

"That's what this is. An older technology," Katherine said.

Jeffrey raised his hand and cut in. "It's not important. But can you share with us how you overcame this obstacle, please?" He pointed to the picture of the wall walker.

"I just . . . messed with it." Ayla looked up. Katherine and Jeffrey stared intently at her. She paused for a moment and contemplated the details she wanted to give them. After all, she wasn't sure how much she could trust them. Her opinion on Katherine changed from one conversation to another, but Jeffrey was a total unknown. "I don't remember doing anything . . . specific. I tried a few things with my crowbar, and then this goo stuff just kind of . . . appeared."

Ayla wanted to ask so many questions, but more than that, she wanted the truth to come out. "Can we keep going? We won't have much time with the camera."

"Prior to this," Jeffrey said again, "what did you observe, or what objects were around you?"

"I'm sure it's on the camera." Ayla leaned over and signaled to Katherine. "Push that button," she said and gestured to the arrow on the right side.

Katherine pushed the button.

"Keep going." Ayla watched the images. "Stop!" She didn't mean to raise her voice, but the display showed a scrambled, blurry image of the circular marker on the ground in the abandoned building. "I'm not sure what corrupted these, but this"—she pointed with her face—"is the disc I was telling you about."

Katherine brought the screen closer to her face and then pointed it at Jeffrey. Katherine and Jeffrey whispered inaudibly.

Ayla peered over to where they looked. The screen faded to black, so she tried to reach out and grab it, but it was no use. She sighed, hoping the camera would have enough juice to show them some of her world above ground, but of course, nothing was going her way lately.

"What happened?" Katherine asked.

"It died."

"What do you mean?" Katherine asked again.

"The battery ran out."

"So, we can't see any more?" Jeffrey asked.

"Unfortunately not, but is that enough proof?" Ayla asked. "Do you trust me now?"

What more can they want?

Katherine and Jeffrey turned their backs and had an inaudible conversation of hushed whispers before turning back around.

"Ayla." Katherine lowered the camera and leaned back in her chair. "We're going to have to keep this a bit longer for examination."

"Why?" Ayla asked. "What else do you need to know?"

"I very much appreciate the information and additional detail." Jeffrey ignored the question, stood, and pushed his chair back.

"Katherine . . ." Ayla looked toward Katherine, who was now standing as well, camera in hand.

"Thank you, Ayla. I'll be back, and we can discuss a few more things."

"Am I free to go? Do you believe me now?" Ayla tugged at her restraints and rattled the bed.

Jeffrey's mustache flickered as he let out a chuckle, and Katherine shot him a glance. "I'm afraid that's not up to us," Katherine said.

"What do you mean?"

"Jeffrey and I have to take it to a bigger group."

"What—" Ayla was cut off.

"It's a conversation, Ayla—that's it—about how everyone wants to proceed," Katherine said.

"Who . . . Who's making the call?"

At the door, Jeffrey close behind her, Katherine said, "Don't worry. I'll let you know how it goes."

"Wait!" Ayla shouted but doubted Katherine heard it as the door to her room, and to her freedom, slammed shut once again.

SIX

Leadership

nder ordinary circumstances, Katherine used the library as a getaway, an escape from the mundane day-to-day. She often stopped in front of the oversized two-story oak doors that led to the library. The doors were decorated with inlaid multicolored jewels and engravings.

Multiple times, she had seen people stop and sketch the doors or simply stare and admire them. Today, though, there would be no admiration. Katherine was here on business, not to wander through the stacks and meander around the three-story staircase, browsing for books that looked interesting.

In the far corner of the library, she had squished herself into one of the nooks between a stained-glass window and two large columns. A tattered rug covered the wooden floors and ran past the chairs to where Katherine sat in a folding chair, her back to the rest of the library. She faced the stained-glass window, a colorful picture of an atom rotating around the world. Her focus wasn't on the intricate stained glass but rather on the four people sitting in front of her.

In the chair farthest to her left sat Lee, an eccentric, long-tenured resident and the head of education.

In the chair next to him was Ellen, a scientific leader and head of research.

Beside Ellen was Jeffrey, Katherine's confidant and long-time colleague, who was the head of medicine.

Raymond sat in the last chair, the one farthest to the right. A quiet man, he ran facilities but weighed in heavily on all sorts of cases.

"Thanks for meeting again," Katherine started. "I wanted to make sure we talked about my findings." She looked over at Jeffrey. "About *our* findings as a group, given that we've never seen anyone from the outside before."

"Besides Clay's group?" Lee added with a grin.

"Let me clarify. We haven't seen anyone *unknown* from the outside before." Nods of approval came from the group, so Katherine continued. "Ayla seems to be a special case here. I've followed protocol as much as possible. We did have to set up a bit of a makeshift bed to keep her restrained in the hospital, along with some additional monitoring. Other than an attempted break-out, it seems to be going okay. Thank you to Raymond and the team for that one."

Raymond smiled. "Glad we could help."

"Wait a minute. She attempted to escape?" Ellen leaned forward in her chair.

"We had an unfortunate lapse in judgment by one of our nurses, but we have the situation under control," Katherine replied.

"How do we know she won't escape again?" Ellen crossed her arms.

Jeffrey waved her off. "Ellen, it's fine. I was there."

Ellen looked around at the others. "It doesn't sound fine," she said.

"Can I continue please?" Katherine asked.

The group fell silent. Ellen slumped in her chair.

"Thank you," Katherine continued. "We've seen relatively normal behavior so far—quite the opposite of what I would expect for any foreign agents or spies—and she's been consistent in her story. She's been adamant about her outside life, and we confirmed part of her story with the items from her backpack, primarily her camera."

"Can we see them?" Raymond asked.

"Unfortunately, the camera has lost power, but I plan to get Mr. Fixer working on it again." Katherine cleared her throat and kept talking. "What I'd like to get a consensus on here today is how we go forward from here."

"We bring in Clay, right? He can get the truth out of her," Ellen said.

"We're not torturing anyone, Ellen," Lee said. "If that's what you're suggesting."

"I don't know what Clay's methods are, but Katherine obviously can't get the truth out of her. What, do you want to feed her candy and have sleepovers and promise freedom if she *pretty please* tells us the truth?"

"Encouragement is better than torture," Lee said. Ellen glared at him.

Katherine shook her head and panned across her audience,

already feeling like she had lost some of them. "We have to decide what to do with Ayla. So far, we have been able to follow protocol until we got to the interrogation portion. Protocol says we are to take outsiders to the chamber room and keep and interview them there. However . . ." Katherine looked at the faces in front of her. "Because the chamber room is no longer available to us, we had to get creative." She paused for questions or comments, but surprisingly, there were none. "So, that's when I met with Raymond to rig up restraints and monitoring in the hospital, which we did." Raymond acknowledged her with a nod.

"Can you tell us what you *have* been able to do?" Ellen rubbed her temples.

"That's why I've gotten us together," Katherine continued. "There isn't much else for me to do, from a protocol perspective."

"What does the protocol call for, Katherine?" Lee asked.

"Well, that's my concern." Katherine squinted. "Protocol says I . . ." She corrected herself before continuing. "*We* need to turn her over."

"Turn her over?" Lee asked.

"To security."

"And let Clay deal with her?" Lee's hands shot into the air and landed with a distinct *thud* back on his lap.

Katherine looked up from the ground. "It would appear that way."

"Then what are we waiting for?" Ellen asked. "Sounds like we have a clear direction."

"I don't think protocol makes sense here," Lee chimed in. "Clay is going to torture the girl, and I'm not sure what that gains anybody."

"Ammo and intelligence to fight the war above!" Ellen raised her voice and started to stand. She paused, gathered herself, and sat back down. "Protocol was developed for a reason, and there's no need for us to stray from it."

"That reason is over one hundred years old," Katherine said. "Don't you think things can change over the course of a century?"

"It was written for good reason."

"Maybe. How would we know?"

"Are you trying to sabotage us, Katherine?"

"What!?" Katherine exclaimed.

Raymond jumped out of his chair and wedged himself between the two women. Jeffrey followed suit and grabbed Ellen by the shoulders while Lee stood and did the same for Katherine.

"No need to fight," Raymond said.

"Sit back down. Come on," Lee said calmly to Katherine.

"I'm fine," Katherine replied. "I really am. It's Ellen I'm worried about."

"Why is she even in charge, anyway?" Ellen shouted from across the space behind the chairs. "We can't trust her." She jumped up and pointed, now being held back by both Raymond and Jeffrey, men twice her size.

"Protocol put me in charge. And I've been following protocol. Isn't that what you want?" Katherine said.

"We're a group. We'll put it to a vote," Raymond said. Katherine and Lee nodded along in agreement. "Does that work for you?"

Ellen huffed with her back against the stained-glass window. "Better than a dictatorship, I guess."

Katherine ran her fingers through her hair and adjusted her blouse. Lee pulled his chair around next to Katherine, either to protect her or keep an eye on Ellen, Katherine wasn't sure. She watched as the other two gathered themselves and sat across from Katherine and Lee.

Everyone stared at Jeffrey, who spoke. "It seems our emotional states are in check, yes? If that's the case, I say we proceed with a vote now, unless any other members have input they would like us to field in advance."

"Shouldn't we be getting Clay's input in all of this?" Ellen interjected. "Surely he has a say over something like this."

"I actually don't think we should involve him," Jeffrey replied.

"I agree," Lee added.

Jeffrey continued: "Clay and his team are supposed to be as minimally involved with us as possible, except under the most extreme circumstances."

"I would call this an extreme circumstance," Ellen said.

Jeffrey looked at her with a disapproving eye. "There is actually strict protocol about what constitutes an extreme condition, and this case does not meet those clearly defined criteria." Jeffrey paused, now in charge, which was fine by Katherine, who sat back in her chair and waited to vote. Jeffrey straightened his tie. "Katherine, can we assume your vote is to set her free?"

"Yes. Effective immediately."

Ellen huffed again from across the way.

Jeffrey nodded. "Noted." He turned to the rest of the group. "I guess I will cancel your vote then, because I choose to turn her over, per protocol guidelines."

"What?" Katherine shot back at Jeffrey. "Even after talking with her directly and seeing those pictures?"

"I'm simply following protocol, Katherine."

Katherine sighed as Ellen smiled at her from across the empty space.

"One for Ayla being free, one for her to be turned over." Jeffrey turned to Ellen. "Can we assume your vote is to turn her over?"

Ellen furiously nodded. "Absolutely."

"One for Ayla being free, two for her to be turned over. Lee?"

"I'm with Katherine on this one. I see no reason to turn her over, and in fact, I think that may cause more damage."

"How would it *possibly* cause more damage to follow protocol than let a spy roam free?" Ellen stewed again, her face turning redder.

"I never think torture is a good answer, and from what I'm hearing, she's harmless," Lee replied.

"You don't know anything." Ellen swatted at the air. "Let's get this over with."

"Two votes each way," Jeffrey said.

Katherine squirmed. "Raymond," she said, "you know what should be done."

Ellen glared at Katherine. "Don't try to influence anyone more than you already have, Katherine. You've already done enough damage."

"Ellen . . . please." Jeffrey placed his hand on her shoulder. Ellen slapped it away, so Jeffrey continued. "We can all accept the resolution here. Raymond's vote will determine how we proceed." Jeffrey looked at Raymond, who held his head in his hands.

"Raymond?" Katherine called out.

Raymond panned his eyes across his colleagues. "I don't think I have a choice," he said.

Katherine noticed a hint of a smile run across Ellen's face, while Lee shared a similar expression. Jeffrey's expression didn't change at all. Katherine's heart raced, and her face flushed. She had known Raymond for years, and hopefully his vote wouldn't be a surprise. She watched him lick his lips as he searched for his next words.

"I'm sorry, Katherine." The words fell out of Raymond's mouth.

Katherine's heart sank to the bottom of her chest, and a large pit emerged in her stomach and swallowed her emotions. The lights around her seemed to go dim as she filled in the rest of Raymond's words. He continued, but she didn't hear what he or anyone else said. All she could hear was Ayla's story about how she stumbled onto this place, another case of wrong place, wrong time. Katherine could no longer protect her.

A tear formed in her eye, and she used her remaining awareness to try and hold it back in front of the people she called a family. It seemed silly to care so strongly about a relative stranger, but she couldn't help but feel that the group had made a huge mistake.

"Katherine?" Jeffrey leaned over his associate.

"I'll get in touch with Clay." The words jumped out of Ellen's mouth and bounced around with excitement.

"Wait . . ." Katherine chimed in. "I want to talk to her first. Can I do that?"

Ellen crossed her arms, now standing behind her chair. "Fine," she said. "Thirty minutes is all you get. And Jeffrey's going with you."

"That's fine," Katherine said. She pulled on her sleeve and used it to wipe a wet streak on her cheek. She got up and headed out of the room.

SEVEN

Helping the "Enemy"

Ayla tried to keep her mouth closed as she shimmied her way through the dusty wiring tunnel and followed the man in front of her. Odds and ends of wires and plugs protruded from the walls and brushed against her flimsy hospital garments. Some wires were hot to the touch, and others buzzed when she passed them, so she kept her feet plodding along in the dark and tried not to touch anything. Occasional cracks in the wall let some light shine through, but Ayla mostly used touch to navigate the dark hallway.

Ayla fumbled her way through until the man stopped and started climbing an old metal ladder. She followed him and climbed several rungs until she came to a landing, grabbed the floor, and pulled herself up. The man waited for her, crouched and gasping for air.

"Wh—" she muttered before he put his hand over her mouth. Ayla panted as quietly as her body allowed.

After having tried and failed to escape the hospital, Ayla's hope had been drained. She had been waiting for Derek to burst through the door the entire time, so when someone actually did, she was surprised to see a strange man instead. At first, she was hesitant, but he seemed to offer her the hope she had just lost, so she went along with him.

The strange man had crept in minutes after Katherine had left, and he had an easy time undoing the restraints and finding the right doors and spots to lead them into some kind of utility closet. He had ripped a panel off the back of the closet and exposed this wire-covered hallway they had just wiggled through. The man seemed like he had the route memorized and never hesitated going anywhere, including up the ladder and to their current resting spot.

As Ayla tried to catch her breath, which was easier now with the man's hand not smothering her face and silencing her, she watched as he remained relatively still in front of her. She assumed he was waiting for someone to make noise or indicate they were being followed.

When no signs of life showed up, or rather piqued the ears of her or the man, he looked at her for the first time. His eyes and patchwork beard added youth to his old, worn, and wrinkled ghostly white face. His work boots and frayed jeans cried out that he worked all day, and Ayla had flashbacks of one of the only memories she had of her father.

He made a *follow me* motion with his hands and stood up as much as he could while staying crouched. Ayla close behind, he headed down another hallway in an unknown direction, through more wire closets, cobweb traps, and dusty, rodent-infested walls.

Ayla wasn't sure how long they had been walking, but they came to another landing area with another ladder, but this one led directly into the ceiling. The man quickly propelled himself to the top of the ladder and swung upward with all his weight. His shoulder struck the middle of a plate in the ceiling. He crawled farther up and disappeared into the newly formed hole in the ceiling right as Ayla stepped onto the first rung of the ladder. His buzzed head appeared again in the opening, followed shortly by his weathered and calloused hand.

Ayla and the strange man had reached a small room no bigger than the hospital room they had come from. Scattered cardboard and broken palettes littered the otherwise sparse space. The only items of note were a dusty round table with a chair on either side, a cupboard hanging on the patched wall next to it, and a boarded-up window above the table.

"Here, take a seat," the man said, pulling one of the wooden chairs away from the table. His voice carried an unexpectedly youthful tone.

Ayla gingerly lowered herself onto the fragile-looking chair, her body shaking from exhaustion. The uneven chair shook, making a wobbly noise against the wooden floor.

"This window," the man pointed, "used to look out over the library. I've been told it was a fantastic sight." He headed for the lonely hanging cabinet. "I spend a lot of time up here. Wish that great view was still up here."

"I'm sorry…" Ayla's voice trembled as she spoke. "Who are you?"

"Oh, right. I'm sorry," he said, turning his attention to Ayla. "Thomas."

She stared at him blankly, and he returned the favor.

"Who are you, Thomas?"

He laughed. "I'm here to help you out. You can calm down a bit now, promise. Very few people know this is up here." He swung open the creaky door of the cabinet. "It's an old storage room. There are some old books up here, materials, clothes, supplies, what-have-you."

Though he didn't answer her question, so far, he had more of her trust than anyone else, certainly more than Katherine or Jeffrey. He wasn't trying to lock her up and shackle her to a bed, so that gained him some points.

She didn't want to try and push her luck any more than she already had today. Rubbing her wrists, she cherished that she was at least free from the bed restraints.

"Are there any clothes I can use?" She grabbed her thin hospital dressing. "I'd like something else if you have it."

"Oh, sure. I think that top box is mostly clothes. Whatever you can find."

"Thanks," Ayla said. She headed for a dusty old box on top of the pile. The top of the cardboard was frail, and pieces of it fell off and dropped to the floor when she opened it. Afraid that the box would completely disintegrate, she delicately kept clawing her way through the old clothes. The box stayed intact long enough for her to find something that seemed like it might fit.

Most of the clothes looked old-fashioned, from the fifties or earlier, if she had to guess. She grabbed what looked like patterned capri pants and a basic blue top. Unable to find any shoes, her flimsy hospital standard flats would have to do. "Is there a bathroom or anything?" she asked Thomas, who was now search-ing through the cabinet on the wall.

"Not up here," he said. "You can change behind the stack of boxes." He covered his eyes with his hands. "No peeking. I prom-ise." He smiled, and his attention returned to the cupboard.

Behind the stack of broken crates and soggy cardboard boxes, she found a spot that didn't look like Thomas could see through and started taking off her clothes. "So, what is this place now, Thomas?" she asked, trying to distract him as much as possible.

"It's not used anymore," he said, scouring through the cabinet. "Not since all of storage moved below, anyway."

"How long ago was that?" she asked.

"You know, I'm not too sure . . ."

There was an awkward silence as Ayla put on her shirt and found a place for her old hospital clothes. She decided to put them back into the box.

"Maybe fifty years ago," Thomas said, but it sounded more like a question.

Finished changing, Ayla sat down at the table.

"Good find." Thomas motioned to her new outfit.

"Thanks. It just smells like stale clothes."

"Can't help you there. Still probably better than how I smell." He rifled through the cabinet again. "Sorry about that, by the way." A few wrappers and pieces of paper fell onto the ground. Ayla noted the lack of design on the wrappers, and it seemed like they were generic-branded items. One she was particularly fond of was a gray one with "Candy Bar" stamped across it.

"I didn't even notice. My mind has been elsewhere lately."

"Yeah, you've been through a lot . . ." He reached farther into the cabinet and came back out with a box in his hands. It looked like a cigar box. He flipped the lid open and revealed an off-centered row of what appeared to be tiny frosting-less cupcakes. "They're biscuits," he said. "Would you like some? Probably a little stale." He took one out of the box and popped it into his mouth.

"They're not from fifty years ago, are they?" Ayla laughed, half-serious.

Thomas chewed a little through a half-laugh and swallowed. "They're okay. Not that old. I come up here every now and then. I rotate out the food."

Ayla, who hadn't eaten anything in a while, reached in and pinched one of the four remaining biscuits between her fingers. The half she ate was dry and crumbly, but not terrible. She wasn't used to much more than the soup she had been given, so it was a nice change of pace. The second half she nearly swallowed without chewing.

Thomas reached back into the cabinet and pulled out a stainless-steel mug. He untwisted the top and handed it to Ayla. She quickly grabbed it and drank nearly half of whatever was left in there, which turned out to be water that tasted like dirt.

"There'll be more where we're going. It's not much farther."

With a mouthful of semi-dry crumbs, she asked, "Where *are* we going?"

Thomas sat down and kicked his feet up onto the table. His tattered jeans and work boots sent dust flying everywhere. Ayla grabbed the box of biscuits off the table and set it in her lap. "Well, there's a group of us," he said, "who have been monitoring your situation. Most of us believe you're telling the truth about what's above ground and what's going on."

"You've been spying on my conversations with Katherine?"

"We have connections all over the place."

Ayla swallowed the rest of her biscuit, trying to remember everything she and Katherine had talked about. "Above ground . . ." Ayla trailed off, gathering her thoughts. "Katherine mentioned something about a war. Is that what you're talking about?"

"Yes." Thomas nodded.

"What war?"

"Exactly." He leaned back now and crossed his arms behind his head. "Everyone down here has been told we're advancing technology for the war efforts above, but some of us aren't so sure that war even exists. Now that you're here, we're hoping you can confirm what we've thought all along."

"Okay, hold on." She put her hand up on the table. "Who is this *us*? This group you keep talking about?"

"A collection of people down here, from different areas. We all think we're being lied to."

"Why can't you just leave?"

He laughed. "There's an entire team of security not just trying to keep people like you from finding this place but trying to keep us *in* at the same time. So far, I'd say they're doing a pretty good job."

"I don't remember anyone trying to stop me from getting here in the first place."

"That's why we had to move fast and come rescue you. Protocol says any outsider like you has to be turned over to security. I was lucky to get to you before that happened."

Ayla was lost in confusion again. First it was Katherine's weird questions; now it was everything else. The picture was starting to come together, but it wasn't entirely clear, and it was definitely more complex than she first thought. She tried to fit all the pieces and bits of knowledge together, but her brain refused, like it was trying to compute a complex math equation.

"So, you just want to know what it's like above ground?" Ayla asked.

He swallowed the rest of his biscuit and swooped to grab his water. After taking a swig, he screwed the cap back on and set it down on the table. "Is there a war?"

Ayla stared into his youthful eyes and studied his body language. He seemed eager to learn, hands clasped on the table, eyes wide, leaning forward, receptive to the next words that would come out of Ayla's mouth. Like a kid in school who listened to the most fascinating teacher, he waited patiently for an answer.

She reflected on her time with Katherine and remembered the questions about what was *up there*—and the dismissal of everything Ayla had said. Katherine had automatically assumed she was lying, but Ayla wasn't sure why. Now Thomas stared at her, ready to take her word as gospel truth.

"You said you've been told there's an ongoing war above ground, right?"

Thomas nodded.

"And everyone here thinks that?"

"Everyone but our group," he replied.

Ayla stood in her corner of the room. For once in this place, she had some leverage and decided not to directly answer Thomas's question, wanting to hold out on giving him important information for as long as possible. She started putting the puzzle pieces together.

An ongoing war, an unknown outsider, a mysterious backpack, vague answers to questions. Everything ran through her head again until she stopped mid-stride. Her hands found the top of her head and rested there. The picture became clearer and clearer, and now the words Katherine had muttered what seemed like a long time ago came into focus. *Threat* and *punishment* made so much more sense. "They think I'm a spy."

"Yes," Thomas said. "That's why I had to rescue you." He walked over to her. "Our small group are the only people who believe you're not with the enemy."

"But why rescue me? Why not let them deal with me and send me to security? Why bother?"

Thomas grabbed her by the shoulders, and she stopped pacing. They were face to face, locked in a gaze, and Ayla dropped her arms to her sides as Thomas spoke.

"Ayla, we need your help to escape this place."

EIGHT

Informing Clay

Ellen stomped across the marble walkway and headed straight for the white cross in front of her. She had given Katherine too much leeway, and now it had come back to bite them all.

Speak of the devil. The hospital door opened and revealed Katherine.

"What happened?" Ellen shouted, thirty feet away from Katherine.

"Please . . . keep it down." Katherine's voice sounded weak in the distance. Ellen marched forward.

"Why should I?" She was in a highly visible position and had built a reputation with everyone in the facility. Her tirade through the central square wasn't going to draw any more attention than usual.

"Ellen—" Katherine started to say.

"This is *your* fault." She jammed her pointer finger into Katherine's shoulder.

99

Katherine held up her hands on the defensive. "Ellen, I don't know what happened—"

"You let her out, didn't you? You convinced Jeffrey, somehow."

"We didn't do anything. We came back, and she was gone." Katherine instinctively lowered her voice. "Can we step inside?" Without an answer, she walked back toward the hospital door.

"Why should I trust you?"

"You can ask Jeffrey or any one of the staff who were here when it happened. Check the hospital security logs too."

"You wanted her free. You let her out, didn't you? You do know she's highly dangerous, right?"

Now inside the hospital doors, Katherine raised her voice. "I didn't *want* any of this to happen."

Ellen sucked in air, having hiked across the central square and used most of her energy by spouting off her frustrations with Katherine.

"Jeffrey and I were just walking back from our meeting." Katherine paced. "You were there. It couldn't have been more than fifteen minutes, right?"

"Who helped you?" Ellen jumped in. "It must have been somebody else. A nurse working with you, maybe? Sound familiar?"

"Ellen—"

"I know your game, Katherine. Clay will have to help sort this out."

"Can you please wait to tell him?" Katherine pleaded.

"I have to let him know. She can't be wandering around here."

"Let me track her down before we pull in anyone else—especially Clay."

"You can't handle it, Katherine!" Ellen cried. "You can't!

You've had your chance and it's led to a spy on the loose. What if she steals our technology and takes it all back to our enemies up above? What if you just singlehandedly lost the war for us?" She let out a heavy breath. "Who knows what she's gotten into already!"

Years of scientific research down the drain because we couldn't keep one person contained.

Ellen had worked hard over the years, and now her achievements were threatened by Ayla running loose, potentially hoarding hard-earned knowledge and technology and taking it back to the surface to get reverse-engineered and used against the very people Ellen was trying to protect. Ellen couldn't have her reputation ruined because of some kind-hearted doctor.

Inside, she secretly had doubts of going straight to the top and pulling in Clay, but it was the ultimate power move and possibly one of the only moves Ellen had left.

Ellen watched as Katherine moved her mouth, but she didn't hear any of the words flying past her ears. She didn't wait for Katherine to finish.

"I'm letting Clay know," she butted in. "You can call Raymond or whoever else you need to get help tracking her down, but Clay has to be involved now."

Katherine groaned. "Did you hear anything I just said?" She paused and her eyes fell on Ellen. "Do you really want another incident here? Do you really want Clay's team coming down?"

"We don't have a choice, Katherine. He gets her, anyway. I'm speeding up the process."

"With the potential of harming everyone else."

The two women locked eyes in a stare-down challenge of each

other's intentions. "You know you can't stop me, right?" Ellen finally said.

Katherine sighed. "No, Ellen, I can't." Katherine rubbed her forehead. "I can ask you though, person to person, woman to woman, friend to friend, for some help." Katherine's hands fell to her side, palms up. "Can you help me? I just need some time before we get Clay involved. I can find her. She trusts me."

Ellen stared at the tear forming in the corner of Katherine's eye. *Typical Katherine.*

There wasn't time for emotion in the high-stress world of war they were living in. Everything had to operate efficiently and effectively, just the way Ellen had built her teams. There was a problem in front of them, and they had to solve it, and Katherine's emotions were getting in the way yet again. She had to hold back a smile and almost let slip a chuckle.

"Katherine," Ellen finally said. "I have to bring in Clay. Do whatever you have to do between now and then."

"We have a problem." Ellen slammed her office door, and the windows surrounding it shook.

Her assistant, Sam, bolted upright in the chair he occupied in the far corner of the room. He dropped a book he had been reading and quickly picked it up before setting it on the round wooden table. Ellen reached out to one side of the wall and flicked her wrist. The windows behind her turned opaque and the door locked. She sat behind the large glass desk that occupied one of the office walls. Sam tiptoed toward her, hands behind his back.

"What seems to be the issue?" His quiet voice rose above the noise Ellen was making. The screen embedded in her desk whizzed to life, showing images and text Sam wasn't familiar with. "And how can I help?"

"It's Ayla."

"The outsider?" he asked.

"It seems she's escaped."

"Escaped? How?"

"I don't know yet. Nobody else does either. I had a chat with Katherine." She paused and read something on her screen. "She's looking for her too, but I don't have much hope. Do we still have trails set up on Raymond's cameras?"

Sam shook his head slowly. "Yes, but those have been disabled for quite a while."

"I was afraid of that." Ellen continued typing without looking up. "Can you ask him to set those up again for us?"

"Yes." Sam took a pencil and notepad from his pocket and scribbled a note. Sam was one of only a few who still used pencil and paper. She wasn't sure why he hadn't switched to all-digital like everybody else.

Maybe it's because of his upbringing. The thought flickered in her mind as she kept scrolling through screens.

"He'll probably get asked by Katherine too," Ellen said. "Make sure she doesn't know we have an in with him as well."

"I'll make it clear with him." Sam kept scribbling. "Do you want me to run it by Lee?"

Ellen paused at her desk. She had taken Sam under her wing after his parents died in the infrastructure incident when he was fifteen. If she hadn't taken Sam in, he would have ended up in the central square peddling whatever supplies he could get his hands on, and she'd thought he deserved better than that. She wasn't sure why she'd felt that way on that particular day, but as time went on, she realized it was nice to have someone appreciate her intelligence and do what she asked.

Sam was young and had a lot to learn. He knew about Clay and the history of the person who occupied the head-of-research position before her, but today, she didn't feel like giving him a history lesson on the entire facility, including Lee's involvement.

She looked up at him. "That won't be necessary. However," she continued, "I'll need to meet with Clay." Ellen punched a virtual button popping out of her desk, and the opposite wall spun to life. Sam flinched. Ellen stood, adjusted her shirt, and walked over to the section of the bookshelf that was now dissolving and revealing a two-foot-by-two-foot screen. Ellen stopped in front of the screen and spoke over her shoulder to Sam.

"Stay out of the shot." She made a shooing motion with her hand, and Sam stepped back until he bumped into the wall. He froze in place.

The screen flickered slowly, then faster until it went all white. After a brief flash, the screen dimmed, and a man appeared. Ellen recognized him, but it wasn't who she was expecting.

Ellen and Raymond and their respective positions were the only ones allowed to directly communicate with the external security team. Raymond was in charge of coordinating supply drops—like food and medicine—and Ellen was in charge of keeping them apprised of their latest technology developments.

"I need to speak to Clay," she said to the man on the screen. "Privately."

"He's not currently available." The man's voice sounded low on the old black-and-white screen.

Ellen sighed. "When *will* he be available?"

"You can wait for him, if you'd like."

"It's extremely urgent."

The man's facial expression didn't change. "You can wait for him, if you'd like."

"How long?" Ellen cocked her head to the side.

"I don't know that information, but you can wait for him, if you'd—"

"Fine. Open the door, please."

"Passcode?" he asked.

She stepped closer to the screen. "Seven. Nine. Eight. Eight. Alpha One. Uniform Nine. Romeo One. Alpha Four." She stated the words in a low voice, careful to enunciate each syllable.

"One moment." The man turned to the side and stepped forward, half on-screen and half cut off.

Ellen waited and tapped her foot. She turned to Sam. "If I'm not back in thirty minutes, call them and let them know."

Sam jotted something in his notebook. "Okay," he said weakly.

Ellen strongly disliked walking through the lower levels, so one of her first tasks was to install a portal in her office, which took her to the external supply room, where the outside supplies entered the facility. In rare cases, she'd meet Clay in this room.

The man fully reappeared on the screen, and then the space on the shelf next to the screen disintegrated and revealed Ellen's supply room portal. She stepped toward it, and as she reached the boundary, stopped momentarily. "Thirty minutes," she said before stepping into the portal and disappearing from her office.

* * *

The other side of the portal opened into a room six times the size of Ellen's office, with another floor stacked on top. It was big enough to store most supplies until they had time to retrieve more when they ran out.

The halogen lights beamed from above and bounced off the exposed polished concrete floor. The rest of the room was covered in crates stacked five high in areas and containing everything from food, clothes, and medical supplies to the technology asks Ellen had in for her team. Some crates were cracked open. Others were shoved into the corner, having gone untouched for years.

The only open space in the room was near the front, close to the portal doors. There was a sole chair in the area, pushed up against a small table, so Ellen sat down, crossed her legs, and fidgeted with her foot. Her fingers tapped against her knee, and if she had gum, she'd be chomping away at it, but gum was a luxury, and she hadn't had any in months.

The room had no windows and only one rather large door against the far wall. It was welded shut. No surprise to Ellen, given how far they had come with teleportation. Portals were used everywhere and were adopted quickly. Regular doors and older transportation mechanisms had limited use anymore. The door in this room was one of the first to be replaced by a few portals.

There was one large one for the supplies to come through and two Ellen used to travel down here and back. The last two were against the opposite wall. Clay used one to come in and another to go out. Ellen stared at the entry and exit doors, frustrated that she hadn't yet cracked the code of two-way portals. It was an unfortunate inefficiency to use two doors instead of one, and it bothered her every day.

There was also another exit point next to Clay's two portals: an older wall walker door that Ellen was quite fond of. She had been on the team that cracked that code, and it helped propel her to her current position.

She stared ahead, tapping her shoe on the floor. She hated being in this position—having to bring this type of information to Clay. But she also loved being the only one able to do it in the first place. She wasn't sure exactly how Clay would react, mostly because he was unpredictable.

Ellen adjusted her position on the uncomfortable chair when a loud noise came from the opposite wall. Clay stood tall, having just come through his entry portal. Ellen cracked her knuckles, shook out her arms, and stood up.

He looks calm. She walked over to him with her hand extended.

Clay approached with his hands behind his back. He scowled and paced around her. "I'm busy, Ellen. What is it?"

She dropped her hand to her side and turned to face him again. "I wouldn't be bothering you if this wasn't important."

Clay had wandered over to one of the crates by the table and ran his finger across the top. A poof of dust fell onto the floor.

Ellen waited for his response, but when none came, she continued. "I have an update on the outsider."

"Go on." Clay had his back to her.

"She's no longer in custody."

Clay ran his finger all the way down the crate and flicked it off the end and into the air. He sighed and started talking before he turned around. "Ellen, do you know how long I've protected this place from the outside world?"

"Not exact—"

"How long I've kept this facility away from the war? How long I've guarded you and your people?"

She paused, waiting for him to finish or to clarify his rhetorical questions, but after enough time had passed, she chimed in. "A long time—"

"Over twenty years." His gaze now lifted upward, and his blue eyes peered through Ellen.

She was struck by his paleness and the exaggerated sharpness of his cheekbones in the overhead lights. He had certainly looked better in the past, but Ellen assumed he was dealing with so many things she knew nothing about that she couldn't understand his situation completely.

Clay continued. "In those twenty years, do you know how many incidents I've had to deal with?"

Ellen tore her eyes away from his bright blues, which seemed to have a grip on her. She concentrated on the corner of the room. "I just know of the one, sir."

"That's right," he said. "Just the one." He kicked his foot at invisible dirt on the ground. "The one that forced out your mentor and predecessor. The one that cleared Michael out of here and put you in power. The one that got everyone in this godforsaken facility back on track and reminded them of their place in the war." A smirk ran across his face. He flashed his eyes at her again. "That's the kind of influence I have over this place. You know that, and my bosses above know that."

Ellen nodded in affirmation.

"So let's get to the heart of the matter." He seemed to glide across the floor and found his way next to Ellen. While not physically intimidated, she tensed as he approached. "You and I, Ellen, we want the same thing." Ellen's face must have given away some of her thoughts. Clay stopped and laughed. "No, really," he said. "We do."

"How . . . how so?" she mustered up the courage to ask.

"Well, we can't have a spy on the loose trying to expose us and steal our secrets. If she gets back to the top, she'll give the upper hand to our enemies."

Ellen nodded again.

"So, I could do what I did last time," he said. "Put together a team, infiltrate the facility, find Ayla, displace anyone who has been helping her, and we'll all carry on our merry way."

"I would think so, yes."

"But the fallout would be less than ideal, don't you think? What would everyone else down here say about Clay coming in and busting heads again like he did last time?" He circled Ellen again. "The rebellion lasted a long time after that, didn't it? We didn't get all the doubters, did we? This place was still not as tidy as it needed to be, right?"

"That's fair, yes," Ellen said.

"And last time you and your team rolled out teleportation to distract everyone." He stopped in front of Ellen and stared at her. "Do you have anything like that this time, in case we need to entertain the masses?"

Ellen's memory reached back fifteen years. Her predecessor, Michael, wouldn't give portals to Clay, so he put Ellen in his place. She handed Clay the technology without hesitation to get on his good side—she wanted nothing to do with his bad side. There were kinks to work out, like with any new technology, but it united the facility after a tumultuous time.

"We should have two-way portals soon, sir. But nothing quite as revolutionary, no."

"So, *you* don't want me to step in and clean up, right? Because if you have nothing to squelch riots, then what good are you to me? If I have to clean up again, I can't promise you would make it out unscathed." He grinned. "I don't want to do that, Ellen. I actually like having you here."

She gulped. Clay was as ruthless of a person as Ellen had ever met, so she didn't doubt that he was willing and capable and probably enjoyed inflicting pain on others.

"So, you see, we really do want the same thing." At the external portal, he turned to face Ellen, who now stood in the middle of the room, alone, wringing her hands. "Just to be clear, what I'm proposing here is to have you take care of it." He stood, stone-faced, smile and laughter gone, staring at Ellen.

She heard "proposal," but she didn't think that was the right word. A proposal usually implied each party had opted in or had a say in the matter. A proposal was more of a suggestion, and Clay was not suggesting anything today; he was mandating it. He had decreed it, and she had to follow through. She had to get rid of Ayla and clean up this mess.

"Understood," she said.

"Excellent." His smile returned. "Our little deal worked out well last time, right?" Without giving her a chance to respond, he continued. "I know you'll be able to handle this too."

Before the words hit Ellen's ears, he walked through the second portal, next to the one he had come in from. The metal door slammed into the ground, locking access to the only portal that led to the world above.

NINE

Eden

"I don't know how I can help you escape," Ayla said, pacing in the small corner of the room. "I barely know where I am."

"You know about the outside world."

"But I don't know how to get there from here!"

"Leave that to us."

"And the *us* you keep talking about? I have no idea who that is. I hardly know what's going on, Thomas. I know a total of two people in this whole damn place."

"That's fine," Thomas said, placing the stainless-steel mug into the cabinet before walking over to one of the bare walls. "You're about to meet everyone anyway."

"What do you mean?" she asked.

"The group I keep talking about, you want to meet them, right?"

"Of course, but—"

"I suppose you don't really have a choice, do you?" Thomas slid one of the broken crates out of the way and revealed a slightly off-color patch on the wall, like a spot where a painting had been hanging for a long time but had been removed some time earlier. He reached over and peeled off the section of the wall, which must have been a panel of some kind. Behind the panel was a glowing red gel-like spot. Ayla's memories flashed back to what was behind the WW-8 door, where this weird adventure started. "You can go back the way we came if you want, but I wouldn't recommend it."

"What is that?"

"Do you trust me?" he asked.

Ayla stepped toward the stranger. "Not really." She took his hand.

"Good enough for me." He took one big step and leaped straight into the wall. Ayla had no choice but to follow him. She was pulled along, closed her eyes, and instinctively held up her free hand. Her skin tingled, and she became very cold. Before her brain had time to process it, she opened her eyes and found herself holding Thomas's hand. She was now in a dark, very narrow hallway and grasping at the wall to keep herself from falling over.

"It's a portal," Thomas said.

Ayla stared at him. "What?" she asked, staggering against the wall to find her bearings.

"You asked what it was. It's a teleportation portal."

"Teleportation?" Her head spun and a warming sensation rushed over her. She was actively living in a science fiction movie, and she was sure she'd wake up from this wild dream any minute. Between her experience with Katherine and the goo and traveling through walls, she questioned what was real anymore. Without warning, a sharp pain shot through her skull, and she winced and grabbed at her head.

"Are you okay?" Thomas asked, stepping toward Ayla.

She closed her eyes, took a few deep breaths, and waited for the pain to go away. When she opened her eyes, Thomas was staring back at her.

"That was how I got in," she said.

"What?" Thomas asked. "Are you going to be okay?"

"I'm fine," she said. "I found one of those portals to get in. It was under an old abandoned building."

"Just . . . sitting there?"

"No," Ayla said. "It was behind a door."

"Hmm," Thomas muttered. "Watch your step—there's no electricity here, just those dim lanterns."

Ayla followed Thomas's pointing hand to an old gas lantern clinging for dear life to an old, rotting two-by-four providing minimal structural support. As they made their way down the hall, the two-by-fours became evenly spaced between the dirt walls, and they were all in a different state of disrepair. Ayla shuddered each time she passed one.

"Are we safe here?" she asked.

Thomas kept moving forward and took a while to respond. "Safe enough," he finally said.

Ayla sweated and her breathing quickened as she and the strange man went into the dark tunnel. She was comfortable being uncomfortable, having raised her brother mostly by herself and figuring out things a child shouldn't worry about, but this situation was entirely different. Being underground made her even more grateful for her mother's sacrifices.

"You still back there?" Thomas's voice called out ahead.

Ayla realized she had been dragging her feet. She picked up her pace and caught up. "Yep." As she passed, she reached out and touched one of the supporting beams. A few splinters cracked off and fell to the dirt floor. "How much farther?"

"Not much."

Always something to look forward to.

It had always been a matter of *just around the corner* for her, and she found it ironic that her lot in life hadn't changed, even if she was in some quasi-futuristic underground world.

Growing up in a small town, she had always thought *When I get out of here* . . . And then she finally did.

Then it was *When I find a job* . . .

And then *When I settle down with life* . . .

Time passed without answers to her ongoing questions. She found herself in a new place in life but continually waiting for the next thing just around the corner, sometimes in a literal sense, like guiding herself down a dark hallway.

Did Derek feel the same way?

Her body ached every time she thought about how she had left him, and the pangs of hurt ran through her chest; she purposefully didn't tell him her plan. She wished she could yell all the way up to their apartment, call Derek to her exact location, and wait for him to sweep in and end her nightmare. It wasn't a possibility, but an anger continued to build inside her. Anger that she was stuck again, anger that she was trapped, anger that she couldn't do much of anything.

Until she could figure out how to help Thomas and whatever mysterious group lay around the corner, she would have to continue to wait, and the fire inside her kept rising.

* * *

After some time, they came to an oversized oak door decorated with ornate carvings. Near the top of the door, stars swooped over a large snow-capped mountain. A fire raged in the foreground next to images of a stream, deer, and birds.

"What is this?" she asked.

"Step back." Thomas ignored the question. He knocked five times at head height, where the mountain met the sky, then pulled his hand away and waited. A clicking sound came from the top of the door, followed by another at the bottom. Another noise came from behind the slab of oak, like the inner workings of a grandfather clock clicking and ticking away. There were two more clicks on the side, and then the door swung open.

Ayla shut her eyes as the light from the room escaped and flew down the once-dim hallway. She squinted as Thomas grabbed her elbow and escorted her forward.

The first thing she noticed was the grass under her feet. It poked up and through her thin hospital shoes, and the individual blades stabbed her soles. After having been tied to a bed, it was an incredible feeling. It brought her back to the days of running through her backyard, forgetting about the problems in her family's life.

She tried prying her eyes open but didn't see more than a bright light and shades of the green grass below her. Thomas pulled her toward a blurry white object. They walked through a flimsy piece of plastic, like something inside of a carwash. Once inside, the light dimmed, and Ayla cracked open her eyes. She stood inside of a white tent with long tables along the sides. A man in the middle of them stared back at her.

"Hi," he said, striding forward to meet Ayla and shake her hand. "I'm Lee." He looked over at Thomas. "Thanks for bringing her here safely."

"Only a little bit of excitement," Thomas said.

"Excellent," Lee said. "I think Ayla and I have a lot of catching up to do. Can you wait outside?" He asked Thomas.

"I'll be there if you need me." Thomas left through the tent flap.

Ayla couldn't grasp what was happening.

Am I outside now? Or still underground? Who is this weird man with the beard? Is this the group *Thomas talked about? Why is he more tanned than the others?*

So many questions ran through her head that she felt like they might be visibly spilling out of her ears.

"What's going on?" Ayla blurted.

Lee laughed. "A fair question, a fair question."

"Who—" Ayla started to ask.

"Can I ask you something?" he interrupted, sitting in a nearby folding chair. He paused, but not long enough for Ayla to answer. "Is the world at war?"

Ayla paused, taken aback by the abruptness of Lee's question and the quirkiness of his mannerisms. She thought about turning around and running away, hoping she was outside and hoping she could run to somewhere familiar. The only thing that stopped her was Thomas's words about life underground and why the group he kept talking about existed in the first place. Lee seemed mostly harmless, and she *did* want to figure out what was actually happening here, so she engaged, remembering Katherine's comments from earlier.

"The war you're building technology for?" Ayla replied.

"That's the one."

She hesitated, thinking about possible leverage, but decided she had to get answers first. "No," she said and took a seat in another folding chair next to Lee. "There's no war. The technology you have here, the portals—I've never seen them before."

Lee laughed again, a higher-pitched chuckle. His long, graying beard shook every time his mouth moved. He slapped his knee. "That's exactly what I thought." His laughter died out, and he adjusted his glasses and pushed them up his long nose.

"You don't seem surprised. Are you part of that group trying to get out of here?"

"Yes, exactly!" Lee said. "Thomas must have had a lot to say about it."

"I wouldn't say a lot . . ." Ayla's voice trailed off. Her tongue rolled around her dry mouth.

"We don't think there's a war, or at least not anymore. We'd like to explore your world, but we're being held here against our will."

"By who?" Ayla asked.

"Well, that's a good question, isn't it? I don't know. Do you?"

Full of confusion, Ayla stuttered. "I-I'm not sure?"

"Oh, that's all right. I didn't expect you to know. I was just curious."

"I've heard about security before . . ." It wasn't a question or a statement. She just wasn't sure exactly what Lee was looking for.

"Oh, no, they've been around forever, as far as I know. I believe they were first part of the United States government, but I'm not so sure anymore. It doesn't seem like the government would lock us away down here and forget about us." Lee scratched his chin.

"I'm sorry," Ayla chimed in again. "I'm confused."

Lee's high-pitched laugh rang out through the tent once more. "Oh yes. Quite, quite, I imagine."

"I . . . don't know who everyone is and who I can trust, you know?"

"Sure," Lee replied, nodding. "So, tell me . . . can you trust me?"

"I don't know."

"Well, I can let you in on a little secret." He leaned in and lowered his voice. "I'm the main reason you're out of your holding cell and that you're here right now. I helped free you." He leaned back in his chair, a wide smile across his skinny face.

Ayla let the words hang in the air before replying. "How?"

"I can control a few things." He crossed his feet, and for the first time, Ayla realized he was barefoot. Her face must have given it away, because Lee laughed again and spoke up. "I'm sorry. I hope this doesn't bother you. I just love the feel of grass between my toes."

"No, that's okay," she said quietly.

"Anyway, I was saying . . ." He scratched his beard. "Oh, right. I'm part of leadership here. We make decisions about everything: portioning out rations, when to make announcements, who should—"

"Is that the group Thomas was talking about?"

"Heavens no. That's just who runs the logistics of our *little* facility." His long fingers air-quoted the word. "The group you're talking about is much smaller, and we operate out of this place." Lee waved his arms around. "Not the tent, but . . . You know what? Let's go take a look." He stood and headed for the entrance. "Oh, and by the way—" He turned and had a smile on his face. "It's a *secret* group."

"Got it," Ayla said and followed him out through the tent.

LYING BENEATH

* * *

Ayla shielded her face with her arm. Her eyes didn't take as long to adjust this time, and once they did, she lowered her arm and found herself looking out onto a lush, natural landscape of rolling hills with vibrant green grass and several trees popping out of the soil.

A stream ran through the middle of the room and ended in a pond near the entrance, where they now stood. A giant orb of light hung from the ceiling, like a delicate chandelier. Everything was organic and natural, other than the tall metal walls defining the outside border of the room. Ayla found herself looking at a Garden of Eden landscape, a perfect place trapped in a metal box underground. Then she noticed the people: kids playing in the grass, others swimming in the nearby lake or hauling supplies, and a few simply lounging. It was a far cry from the sterile hospital environment she had come from.

"What is this place?" she asked.

"A long-forgotten room of the past," Lee said. "Previously used to study natural sciences and dabble in magical sciences." Lee curled his toes around blades of grass. "It was abandoned a long time ago to get more people to focus on . . ." Lee paused. "More *hard* sciences, I would say." He looked around and breathed in the fresh air. "I found out about it while searching through some older history books in the library. As soon as we physically found it, I knew it'd be a perfect hiding place for our group, in case anything was to happen. Of course, we had to make a lot of changes due to the malfunctioning sunlamps, the new portals, and how rundown the place was . . ." A long sigh escaped his mouth. "But I digress. We've been gathering here since you arrived."

"Everyone is part of this . . . faction?" Ayla asked.

"Yes."

"Even the kids?"

"Yes. There are only forty-six of us, Ayla. Out of about seven hundred people here in the facility. We're not much of a force to be reckoned with."

"Why aren't more people with you?"

"Why would they be?" Lee asked. "They don't know any other way of life. They're indifferent."

"But how can they just not care if they're being lied to?"

"Some people don't think that. There are still a lot of people who think they're fighting for the good side in an imaginary war. There are a lot of people who are neutral too. They don't really care one way or another."

They strolled over to the pond. Ayla soaked in every minute of the fresh air and sunlight. Then she paused, mid-stride. Lee didn't notice until he was a few paces in front of her.

"Fresh air. Sunlight," she said and pointed up toward the orb in the sky.

A big smile ran across Lee's face. "One of the benefits of technology. We pipe all that in. Technically, we teleport it in, but either way, that's how we get it in here." He pointed up at the ceiling. "Our giant sunlight portal."

"But it's coming from the outside," Ayla said.

"We've worked in secret to get access to what we need."

"It's just like the portal Thomas and I used to get here? That weird red, squishy wall?"

Lee laughed. "Yes, it is. Although this one is less squishy and red."

"Hm," Ayla muttered to herself. She wasn't sure what to think as she caught up with Lee.

"A lot to take in, I imagine," he said. "Take your time. We'll take a stroll around the lake. Feel free to ask me anything you'd like."

Ayla swore she heard birds chirping off in the distance and saw a couple of squirrels running across tree branches, but it could have been her imagination. She missed the outdoors, the smell of the grass, the coolness of the autumn breezes above, and she realized the people living here—underground—didn't know what they were missing out on: walking dogs through city parks, reading a book in the warmth of a sunny day, running through fields without a care in the world.

She felt a twinge in her chest, an achy pain. It wasn't physical; it was an emotional pain she felt not for herself but for everyone here. Compared to them, she wasn't stuck at all; but everyone else was—and in a worse way. Ayla and Lee walked in silence halfway around the lake before she had anything to add to the conversation.

"This is what the world is like." She pointed upward. "Up above."

"I knew it!" Lee exclaimed. "All the more reason to get out of here."

"I want to help," she said. "I want to get people out of here. Get them back to the real world."

"Excellent." Lee's smile grew larger. "We've been developing our plans and are expediting now with you here."

"A plan to escape?" Ayla watched people milling about across the pond.

"Exactly, yes," Lee said. "We're stuck here, and we can't wait for anyone to help us. We have to do it ourselves."

Ayla scratched her head. "If I'm hearing right, the government is keeping you down here?"

"Well, technically, the security group is. But I'm sure there's someone up there telling them what to do."

"Who *is* the security group?"

"Good question," Lee said, tiptoeing around a cluster of slippery rocks. "They protect us from the outside and keep us in. Clay heads up that division, and in fact, they are the ones you're supposed to be with now. Remember how Katherine said she was trying to help? She was trying to protect you from them—from *him*, specifically."

"He's not a good person?"

Lee smirked. "Him or his team."

It made sense that there'd be a security force, but it seemed surprising that Clay wouldn't know about the entrance Ayla had used. It wasn't hidden or anything. "Why didn't they stop me when I found that door? How was I able to get past them?"

"They must not have known about it." Lee shrugged. "I bet they fixed it now though," he added with a laugh.

They circled the pond and headed back to the tent. Thomas appeared over a slight hill, jogging their way. Lee picked up his pace, and Ayla followed. The three met halfway up the hill. Thomas was sweating and panting, his eyes bulging out of his head.

"I think . . . we have . . . a problem." He was out of breath and sucking in air.

Lee grabbed him by the back of his arm. "What is it?"

"Clay and security . . . they have Ayla's boyfriend."

All the blood rushed out of Ayla's face.

Light-headedness.

Tingling arms.

Her legs twitched.

The sound around her dropped out, and it all became a low buzzing.

Lee's and Thomas's faces faded in with the background. The world around her blurred. Her breathing became faster.

They had Derek.

Is he okay?

The thoughts ran through her mind faster than she could comprehend them.

Is he—was he trying to rescue me?

Did he come after me?

Is it—am I the reason he got caught?

Is he hurt?

Can I—where is he?

How is he?

Where is he? Where is he?

"Ayla, please try to calm down," Lee said in a soothing voice. She wasn't sure if the questions had been in her head or stated out loud.

"Where is he?"

"Ayla . . ." Lee set his hand on her shoulder.

Ayla swatted his hand away and turned to Thomas. "Where is Derek?"

"I don't . . . exactly know," Thomas replied.

"Is he safe? Who has him? Can we help him?" Her words fell out of her mouth, like she had taken a too-big sip of water and couldn't hold it in anymore.

"Where is he?" Her mind focused on the last thought, and she blurted it out. The blurry face in front of her started to resolve into a clearer image.

Lee tried to cut off her overflowing words. "You have to get back in control and listen to me."

"He's somewhere in the lower levels of the facility, below the central square," Thomas said. "We think."

Ayla didn't know what any of that meant but trudged forward anyway. "How do we get there?"

"It's . . . not quite that simple," Lee said.

"Why not?"

"That area is large and expansive. Even if we knew exactly where he was, it would take us a while to navigate." Lee paced. "And even if we knew all of that, Clay and his men have him. We can't out-muscle or sneak around Clay."

"We have to go rescue him!" Ayla stomped off toward the engraved oak door. If nobody else would help her, she'd have to do it herself.

Lee grabbed her by the arm and spun her around. "Ayla, you can't rescue him by yourself. It's incredibly dangerous."

"I don't care." She shook her arm loose and stomped off. Thomas ran in front of her and blocked her path.

"What, are you taking me prisoner now?" She turned and headed for Lee and raised her voice. "This isn't any better than when I was locked in that room. Why do you—"

"We can't just run off and play heroes."

"Why not?" Ayla insisted. "We have to. We need to—"

Lee held up his hand and cut her off. "We have a plan."

Ayla stopped. Thomas's arms were crossed like a bouncer, and she waited for a response from Lee. After not hearing the plan, she threw her hands up again. "Well, what is it? I won't hesitate to go get him myself."

"You don't even know where he is."

"Neither do you," Ayla interjected. "Why can't we just ask?"

"What are we supposed to say? 'Sorry, Clay, but this person from the outside would like to leave now'?"

Ayla stared up at Lee, went to open her mouth, but quickly closed it, knowing she didn't have anything else to add.

"Clay's entire life purpose is to keep strangers out and keep us in. It isn't something he can be talked out of."

"You're saying you live under a dictator?"

"In a way, yes. And if you hadn't noticed, we don't have weapons, but he does."

The thought hadn't crossed Ayla's mind, but in the time she had been down here, she had not seen a weapon and had only been stopped by sheer force or manpower.

"We're pretty free," Lee added. "He doesn't meddle much in our business, and we don't get in his way. That's why this is so problematic, you see? We've tried to fight back a bit in the past. Fifteen-ish years ago. Word got around fast and got us into trouble, so this time we're being more careful."

"What do you mean it got you into trouble?"

"With Clay. That was the one time he *did* meddle with us. I was lucky enough to escape."

"Escape what?"

"The fallout. Most people in the faction were identified. Some of us weren't." He eyed Thomas, who stood guard. "My predecessor was not one of the lucky ones."

"Your predecessor was part of a faction? What happened to him?" Ayla asked.

"Yes. He and others mysteriously disappeared. Last I saw him, he was being dragged around by a bunch of guards."

"And you're okay with that? You didn't fight back?"

"Wasn't a point to it then. We weren't well-organized, and it was mostly a spark and a bunch of smoke. No real fire, you know? But *now* . . . Now with the technology, we think we're better off. And we're hoping we can use your knowledge to help us navigate the world outside of here. We're not meant to live like this . . . I can feel it."

"We can help you get out. And we can share the story with the world. They'll want to know the injustices going on down here," Ayla said.

Lee smiled. "I just want to make sure we get out safely."

"And I want to make sure everyone else gets out," Ayla said. "So, what *is* the plan? You're in charge, right?"

He lowered his voice and chuckled. "We've found a way to reverse a teleportation portal."

"So, those portals, those ones we used to get here—they only go one direction?"

"Correct."

"And some go to the outside?"

"Not quite. Remember when we were talking about this portal?" Lee pointed at the sunlight above. "There are some that stream in sunlight and air, and those *come from* the outside. We've figured out how to travel through them and get ourselves to the outside world."

"Well, can't you just go through that one then? What are you waiting for?"

"Unfortunately it's not that simple."

Ayla wasn't going to argue anything scientific, so she quickly changed the subject. "But they *do* go to the outside? Do you know where?"

"Best we can determine, they can't go farther than one hundred miles. We're kind of hoping you can help us there."

"Within one hundred miles, it could be almost anything." She paused. It could even be her hometown. It had always felt like the middle of nowhere when in actuality it wasn't more than a forty- or forty-five-minute drive into town. "My guess is they'll have most of the portals set up in an out-of-the-way type of place, probably rural land near the city, but far enough away to avoid suspicion. Maybe disguise it as farmland or an unused acreage or something."

"Excellent!" Lee jumped into the air. "As long as we're not setting ourselves up to be airdropped somewhere dangerous."

"Shouldn't be," Ayla said, thinking of all the desolate farmland she was familiar with. "But what about Derek?"

Lee cleared his throat. "I think we can get him out too."

"You *think*?" Ayla raised her hands in the air. "I've been in pure hell in this place and I'm ready for it to be over. I need reassurance, Lee. I need to know Derek will be safe and I'll be safe with him and we'll be able to get out of here . . ." She covered her face. It was all she could do in this situation all by herself. Derek had sacrificed so much by trying to rescue her, so she had to try and rescue him.

"I get it, Ayla. I do," Lee said. "I will personally make sure Derek gets out safely, okay?"

Ayla looked him square in the eyes. "I'm going to hold you to that."

TEN

Taken and Questioned

*** Two Days Prior ***

Derek slammed into the side of the confined space. He had been trying to track down Ayla and found himself captured and bouncing off the walls of a claustrophobic box and going wherever his captors wanted him to go. Every now and then, he called out for help, hoping anyone would hear him, but his voice started fading, and he quickly used up his energy.

He started out trying to memorize every twist and turn in order to reengineer his escape later, but it was a long journey, and he missed a few. He gave up after what seemed like hours in the tiny space. He finally came to a rest and tried to peer through the bottom of the bag over his head but couldn't.

There were no murmurs of outside voices.

There were no bangs or clanks.

It was quiet, and he was alone in his box.

Thinking about Ayla, he hoped she hadn't suffered the same fate. He couldn't imagine her having to go through this, and he felt guilty for letting it happen.

I should have seen it coming.

He should have given her what she wanted and taken her back to the abandoned building instead of letting her sit around and wait. He should have led the charge. He should have done a lot of things differently. His guilt turned into anger, and heat radiated from his face.

Why did she leave in the first place?

She could be impulsive, sure, but sneaking out in the middle of the night without telling him or warning him rubbed him the wrong way.

The silence was broken by a clicking noise, followed by sounds of shuffling outside the box. Before he realized what was happening, the bag over his head was pulled off, and the searing light of the outside world hit his eyes. He squinted at the dark figures hovering above him and lifting him to his feet. The strange figures walked him forward. Derek hobbled across the floor to try and keep up. He counted a few paces before he was thrown into a cold chair.

"Derek!" a voice in front of him called out.

He had to squint to make out the person in front of him.

About ten feet in front of Derek was an unassuming-looking man at a table. He sat cross-legged, stirring a mug of hot liquid, the steam pouring out and billowing toward the ceiling. The man was of a normal stature, build, and height. His hair was blond and kept short, and outside of his fiercely blue eyes, he had the type of face that would blend in with any crowd. Assuming he had no weapons, Derek could easily overpower him and escape. The only roadblock would be his handcuffs.

"I'm Clay." Clay didn't stand up but stared at Derek, presumably waiting for a response.

The room was small, no bigger than twenty feet by twenty feet—a bit larger than a standard jail cell—with three potential exits that he could see: a large sliding door, currently locked shut; an oversized mirror behind Clay; and, in its reflection, a third door in the back of the room.

Standing behind him were also two guards with drawn weapons and decked out in combat-style pants, dark turtlenecks, and multipurpose belts. His attention fell back to Clay with his dark-wash pair of jeans paired with a white button-up shirt and a light brown spring jacket thrown on top. In Derek's years of experience outside the Army, anytime he saw someone who didn't wear the company-standard uniform, it meant they were in charge.

"Why are you here?" Clay asked impatiently, raising his eyebrows.

Derek cleared his throat and tried to conjure up some saliva. "I'm guessing you already know that." His voice was dry and cracked.

"Well, Derek, I'm sorry we have to meet under these circumstances, but I have a good idea." He took a sip from his mug. "I'm guessing you're looking for Ayla?" It came out as a question, but Derek knew it wasn't.

"Is she safe?"

"Yes," Clay said quickly, "but she's not really in my hands." He took another sip.

"What does that mean?"

"It's complicated. All you need to know is she's safe."

"No, I want—"

"You're not in a position to *want* anything, Derek." Clay's cold blue eyes stared through him. "I, however, am. I *want* you to tell me how you and Ayla found this place."

"What do you mean? The building isn't hidden or anything. How do you think we found it?"

Clay gave a look to one of the guards behind him. There were footsteps, then a cold pinch at the back of his neck. It tingled, like a tetanus shot, but it lasted longer. Derek wanted to turn and look, but his entire body froze—from the tips of his toes to his eyes.

His heart pounded, which seemed to be the only thing in his body that moved. He lost feeling in his extremities. The pounding noise grew louder in his head, and his shallow breathing turned raspy.

It felt like an eternity, but eventually, the prickling, shot-like feeling on the back of his neck subsided. The tingling in his fingers and feet faded, and he flexed his muscles, seeing if they still worked. He turned his head back to Clay, who still sat relaxed in the chair, sipping from his mug.

"What the hell was that?" Derek asked, shaking his restrained hands.

"Derek, I can make this worse for you." Clay ignored the question and set his mug down. "How did you find this place?"

Derek sighed. "We were exploring, tried to hide from this security guard in the area, and ducked into this building."

Clay looked at the two guards behind him with an odd expression on his face before turning back to Derek. "How'd you get in?"

Derek licked his lips. "The docking door was open enough for us to roll under it."

Clay scrunched up his face and stared at the floor, like he was pondering a hard math question. "Then what?"

"Then we found a strange symbol on the ground that Ayla was obsessed with." The feeling had returned to his hands now, but he kept wiggling his tingling feet. "She realized it was a handle or something because she could pull on it and stuff started to happen. That's all I know. Tonight, I woke up in bed, and she was gone. I came looking for her and was jumped by you guys. Now I'm here."

Derek felt like he was giving away too much information, but he wasn't in a great position to begin with, and whatever they shocked him with had sent a clear message. While normally Derek would prefer to resist more, he hoped showing them some cooperation would help get Ayla back.

All he wanted was to start over and pretend like this whole experience had never happened in the first place. He still couldn't help but feel angry at his girlfriend for getting him into this position, but that anger wouldn't help him now.

"What did she tell you?" Clay pressed on.

"About what?"

"About what she found."

"Nothing," Derek lied. He hoped what he had given was enough to build some level of trust.

"What were you doing here tonight?"

"I was coming to take Ayla back to our place. Where is she?"

"Why did you let her leave alone?"

"I told you, I was sleeping. I didn't really have a choice. Can I see her?" Derek persisted.

"I told you, you're not in a position to *want* or *get* anything." Clay dropped his mug back on the table. "What else do you know?"

"I already told you everything."

Before Derek could ask any more questions, the familiar black fabric was thrown over his head. He was jostled around again, dragged on the floor, and slammed into walls, and he couldn't tell where he was. His military training kept popping into and out of his head, like a song where you could only hear half the notes.

He didn't know if he was right-side up or upside down at times, and his training failed him, bouncing around his head. At one point, his arms suddenly became weightless, and a feeling of coldness rushed over him. He fell face-first into the ground. A ringing sound echoed through his head, and he lay motionless on the floor, panting, sending dirt into his nose and mouth through the bottom of the bag, which was now half-off the bottom of his face. He didn't care.

It was quiet.

There were no guards around him, no one to pick him up and force him somewhere else. The cold ground cooled his hot, bruised face, and he lay there, waiting for nothing in particular. He caught his breath, and with his hands now free, he removed the fabric from his face. The room wasn't much brighter than his familiar bag, and he squinted to cut through the darkness.

"Hello?" he called out. There was a faint red-tinted light coming through the cracks around a door. Derek could make out dark traces and shadows of what seemed to be a bed on one side of the room and maybe a sink on the other. He searched for a handle at the door or a lock or something but couldn't find one. There were minuscule cracks on the edges, the same cracks that let the light in, but he couldn't see through them.

He pressed his hand against the closest wall and paced around the room, never letting his right hand leave the wall. He walked from wall to wall, around the few obstacles, while feeling each surface and measuring each distance. He found no light switches, no nightstand, no windows, not even a toilet. He was in a prison cell.

Derek sat on the small bed he'd found. The sheets and pillow scratched against him, but it was better than nothing. He leaned against the smooth wall and replayed the events of the night over and over. The hardest thing, other than not knowing where Ayla was or what condition she was in, was his utter confusion about the situation.

Could I have stopped them?

Could I have stopped Ayla?

Should I have pushed Clay harder for answers?

Were these the same guards who spooked us the first night out?

What's with all the secrecy?

His brain asked more questions than he could meaningfully process at a time.

He tried to block out all the thoughts and questions and hung his head in his hands.

He tried to logically think about what he had to do next.

He tried to think of a lot of things, but he couldn't; his mind wouldn't let him.

Staring ahead into the darkness, he smacked his forehead with his palms a few times, wondering what to think of it all, when a tear fell from his eye.

He couldn't remember the last time he'd cried.

ELEVEN

Working Together

llen stomped out of her office, heading to the lower levels. The only reason she typically went to that level was to see Raymond and try to expedite any fixes he was working on for her labs or maybe her office. When she received a confusing, semi-panicked communication from Sam, she determined that she had better see for herself.

The old clunky elevator brought her down to the maintenance level. She shuddered at the use of the old technology. *How did those in the lower levels survive with no teleportation or the other things they had on the upper levels?* She grabbed her sweater and crossed her arms.

All the more reason never to come down here, she thought as the metal doors flung open like a spring, leading her into a dimly lit hallway. The word "Maintenance" was painted on the wall in bright yellow against a dingy maroon wall.

She stepped off the elevator and was blasted by a heatwave.

She let loose the tight grip on her sweater. Her flat soles clunked against the chipped concrete. To the right of the elevator was the quarantine section, indicated by strands of rope and danger signs fashioned together from old sheet metal and crudely welded letters.

She couldn't help but wonder if she could have focused more on infrastructure technology to prevent the failures of her predecessors. It was too late now, and she did end up with a helpful assistant out of it—an assistant she had hoped would be better equipped to handle a situation like this and wouldn't call her down to this level to follow up on something she was sure he could have followed up on himself.

Ellen made her way through the narrow hallway, keeping her elbows tucked in and her hands in front of her. The yellow accent arrows splashed onto the maroon-colored walls led her to the temporary control center, a place where she and Raymond had met before when she couldn't convince him to come upstairs.

At the end of the hallway were two large men who towered a foot over her. She looked them in the eye, and they stared back through their work goggles. They had no weapons, but the hammers and other tools hanging from their belts would work in a pinch.

"Excuse me," Ellen said. With no hesitation, she pushed her way between the men, sliding her elbow under their arms. Sighing loudly, she walked past them, and they stepped back against the wall. She brushed her sleeves off.

"Raymond," she called. "Sam." In the center of the room, the two men were crouched over a screen that rested on a small table with wires running behind and beside it. This command station had all the markings of a temporary operation, including make-shift screens scattered around the room, a mix-and-match set of chairs and tables, and wires running crisscross over the floor. As she approached, the two men turned around.

Sam was flustered, and his hair dripped with what she could only imagine was sweat from the unbearable heat. Raymond was his normal, calm self, his hair carefully parted and slicked to the side. He was decked out in a three-piece suit probably older than Ellen herself. How he wore that all the time she wasn't sure. She already contemplated if she should take off her sweater.

"Why am I down here?" she asked, taking a step onto the platform where the other two men resided.

"We know how Ayla got out," Sam said.

Raymond motioned his head toward the screen in front of them. He moved his hands as he talked and made images appear and disappear at will.

"Ten o'clock this morning," Raymond said. "This is Ayla's hospital room."

The screen flickered and showed a shackle-bound Ayla sitting up in her bed and staring at the wall in front of her. The image lurched forward in a blur before Raymond swished his hands, and it paused again, showing Ayla sitting on her bed.

"Nine after ten," he said, "we see a man enter."

Ellen watched as a man, with his back to the camera, crept in. There was no sound associated with the image, but it looked like Ayla screamed.

"Did anyone in the hospital hear that?" she asked.

"No one we talked to, no. Those rooms are mostly soundproof, anyhow." Sam turned his attention back to the screen.

The man made quick work of the shackles holding Ayla and forcefully pulled her out of the bed and back out of frame.

"Who is that?" Ellen asked.

"Keep watching," Raymond said, moving his arms around again. "We can pick them up again in the hallway . . . there." He pointed as the screen switched to show a different image, and in the top-right, far away from the camera, Ayla and the mysterious man ran down the hallway.

"That's the best image we have?"

"Keep watching." Raymond switched the screen. "We catch them around the next corner again." The image now pointed down another hallway, but this time, Ayla and the man came from the top of the screen and ran toward the camera. Even though the image was grainy and black and white, it had Ellen's attention.

"Is that . . ." The two people on-screen moved closer to the camera before stopping in the middle of the hallway. She watched as the man ripped off a piece of the wall panel and shoved Ayla inside. He then stepped into the hole, and when fully inside, he slid the panel back into place. The scene ended, and Raymond caught Ellen's eye.

"Go back," she said.

Raymond reversed the video to the point right before Ayla and the mystery man entered the wall.

"Stop." Ellen leaned in closer. "It's Thomas." The words fell heavily out of her mouth.

Sam spoke. "We believe so."

"They ducked into a wiring tunnel," Raymond said, retrieving a printed-out blueprint of level one and dropping it onto the table in front of them. "Unfortunately"—his finger traced the tunnel along

the paper—"this wiring tunnel junctions off in at least fifty different directions." His finger indicated such on the map. "And each
one of those has *their* own junction points. It's nearly impossible
to trace."

"So, they could be anywhere?" Ellen mumbled.

"Yes," Raymond said. "We don't have any good indications of
where they went next." He dabbed his forehead with a handkerchief before stuffing it back into his suit pocket. "They don't appear on any other camera system."

"Did you check the library?" Ellen asked, now pacing around
on the platform behind Raymond and Sam. Ellen wasn't sure what
to make of this new information, but she had been around long
enough to learn to follow her instincts.

"Every camera we have access to, yes."

"They have to be there. That has to be their safe house."

"Why do you think that?" Sam asked.

"Lee was one of the only votes to let her free. The library is
his grounds." She glanced at Raymond. "A couple of people want
to set her free, and shortly after we vote, she disappears?" She
scoffed. "Don't you think that's a pretty large coincidence?"

"I was there, Ellen. Lee had his reasons. Nothing seemed nefar-
ious to me." Raymond blotted his forehead with his neatly tucked
handkerchief.

"Let me see." Ellen ripped the blueprints from Raymond's
hands and followed the tunnel paths with her fingers. Raymond
and Sam both took a back seat and watched her from the side-
lines. After a few minutes of tracking down the path options, she
slammed her finger at a spot. "See, there is a tunnel path that leads
directly to the library."

"With all the junctions, you could make a case for any area, even the labs," Raymond interjected.

"What are you saying?" Ellen sneered at Raymond.

"Besides, that's an old supply management room," Raymond said, heading back to the screens. He pulled up another image, a graph with colors on it. "We don't show any power consumption in that particular area. Last confirmed usage was decades ago."

"Sounds like it might make the perfect hiding spot," Ellen said.

"They could be anywhere," Raymond said.

Ellen slammed her fist into the table. "I don't like this." She looked at Sam, who was sulking and taking notes in the corner. "At all!"

Sam dropped his notebook into his pocket and stepped forward. "Actually," he said, addressing Ellen without looking at her. "R-Raymond and I were . . . talking about this b-before you got here. There are a couple of other spots they could potentially be hiding, but . . ." He ran his hands through his hair and dropped his eyes to the floor. "But they're all longshots."

Ellen sensed the confidence building in Sam. "Well then go on," she said, motioning with her hands.

"Well, there are a few spots we know about that aren't used anymore. It's . . . plausible," he stuttered, "that they've commandeered them as hideouts."

"Interesting," Ellen said. "What are they?"

"Well," Sam continued, "the quarantined section down here is a possibility, but highly unlikely."

"Once we had that realization, I sent a few men there looking around," Raymond said. "Nothing spotted."

"Let's not waste our time then," Ellen said. "Other locations?"

Sam continued. "We thought about the storage room too—"

"I've been there recently," Ellen interrupted. "They aren't there. What else?"

"Okay," Sam said. "There's also the abandoned housing floor on level five."

"My office is on level five," Ellen said. "We can look around, but I think that's a wasted effort too."

"That only leaves us with one more spot," Sam said.

Raymond spread out new papers on top of the wiring tunnel blueprint on the table. "A long time ago, before you and I were here, there was another research area."

"Besides my division?" Ellen asked. All of the research went through her. She had never headed up another division before.

"Yes," Raymond said. "I don't know what it was used for, but it's there, nearly isolated from everywhere else." He pointed to a spot off to the side of the map. Ellen initially thought it was a key or legend. "There's a room somewhere in this area. It's almost entirely segregated from us, and nobody is quite sure how to get there."

Ellen leaned in. The map simply showed a square labeled with dimensions and little else. No paths or hallways going to or from the room, and nothing else near it.

"It's completely off the grid too," Raymond continued. "Well, off *our* grid."

"Do you think that could be the spot?" Sam asked.

"I suppose it's possible Thomas figured out how to get there," Raymond said.

"Wait a minute," Ellen said. "Thomas has to have partners." She leaned against the table. "I would bet my life that Lee is in on it too."

"He's got to have read almost every book in the library. Do you think *he* figured out how to get to that isolated area?"

"It's possible," Ellen said. "Either way, we need to find out how to get there."

"I've tried," Raymond said. "And unless I go searching every square inch of this place, I don't know how we'll ever find it." He let out a long sigh. "I don't think it was meant to be found."

"Is there any other information you can give me?" Ellen sat in Raymond's makeshift office now, a separate room behind the walls and screens. A hunk of metal thrown across two sawhorses acted as his desk, and the large, cracked screen behind him flickered with rotating pictures of Ayla's recent escape. Sam was outside at the platform, examining potential escape routes, mapping and comparing energy use, and taking careful notes.

"I've told you everything."

"Even about the old research room? There's got to be something else there."

Raymond didn't move other than to swivel in his chair behind the desk.

"Please . . ." Ellen pleaded.

"I can't get involved. I'm already uncomfortable with the situation."

"Raymond, you're *already* involved. The group voted to turn her over, and now she's running around somewhere."

"That's not my concern."

"It should be. Think of all the damage she could do. She could be plotting right now for something to happen. What if she sabotages our operations or completely destroys our facility?"

"Ellen, she's just one person."

"Working with someone else." She stood up and sent her chair flying back and banging into the wall. "What if Lee's pulled another group together? How can you not be concerned?"

"Because I don't think she's a spy, Ellen," he said blankly from his seat.

His words and stare stopped Ellen in her tracks. Raymond wasn't a particularly intimidating man, but he had a lot of different levers at his disposal. She stood there, gazing at the sweat on his brow, carefully calculating her next move. "Are you one of them? Did Lee recruit you?" she asked.

Raymond sighed, his suit jacket heaving up and down with his breath. "No."

"Then why—"

"If she was a spy, she'd be the worst spy I could imagine." He stood up to be at eye level with Ellen. "She seemingly had no plan coming down here. She knows next to nothing about who we are . . ." He paced behind his desk. "She left all her things with Mr. Fixer, for crying out loud. Even he says her devices are harmless."

His hand waved in the air, and the flickering screen behind him displayed a still-frame image from the earlier footage of Ayla and Thomas escaping the hospital. He waved his arms again, and the image zoomed in on Ayla's face.

"Look at her," Raymond said, pointing at the screen. "Does she look like a top-secret spy or someone who's in way over her head?"

Ellen stared at the image. Ayla's wide eyes bulged out of her head; she was stricken with panic. Her hair was matted and untamable by the best of combs, she dripped with sweat, and the way her body was contorted made it look like she was conflicted between staying in her bed with the devil she knew or running away with the devil she didn't. Ellen had to concede that Ayla did not look like a top-secret spy.

"At this point," she said, "I don't care if she's a tourist or a terrorist." Her gaze turned back to Raymond, who was sitting again in his chair. He was hard to convince, and she had better things to do with her time than suffer down in the lower levels. "I have my orders."

Raymond's eyes lit up. "You talked to Clay about it?" He propped his elbows on his desk. "You have orders?"

"Yes," Ellen said. "We had a nice little chat. I filled him in on the Ayla situation, and he more or less threatened my very existence if I didn't rein this issue in."

"I'm sure he'd be a reasonable per—"

"We're talking about the same Clay, right? You know the horrible things he's done."

Raymond stood up again. "He has a duty to protect us, and whatever he sees as necessary he will do. Believe me." He tugged at his suit jacket, and the edges stretched across his broad shoulders. "I'm familiar with Clay." With a quick swish of his hand, he wiped away the image on the screen behind him. "Is there anything else I can assist with today?"

"You really have no other information for me?"

"Not at this time, no. If I come across anything, you'll be the first to know."

"Remember who's asking me to do this. If he finds out you're blocking progress on bringing in our fugitive . . ." While Raymond was helpful, he was also trying to stay as neutral as possible, and in this case, she didn't need neutral—she needed help.

She would have to formulate another plan with Sam, another angle to take. Now she was running out of angles and, more importantly, time. Clay hadn't given her a timeframe, but after what happened to her predecessor, anything other than *soon* would not work for him. She headed back toward the hallway to the elevator. As she approached Raymond's door, she stopped and turned.

"Goodbye, Raymond."

TWELVE

Ayla's Struggle

Over in the far corner of the Garden of Eden-like room, beyond the lake and sandwiched between two hills, stood an old, towering walnut tree. Lee headed that way, past fields of wildflowers and over dirt paths.

Ayla kept her emotions in check, which was easier now with the newly discovered Mother Nature-inspired distractions. When they reached the base of the hill, a swirling, spiraling staircase carved into the middle of the tree trunk rose up from the ground. Ayla gazed upward, and hidden among the pointy leaves and green, not-nearly ripe walnuts was an old, rickety treehouse perched among the branches.

"It doesn't look like much—" Lee started.

Ayla cut him off. "This staircase is incredible. Who made this?"

"Our group did," Lee said. "All hand-carved. A labor of love."

The carvings that adorned the staircase were delicate and precise. Something like this should be on display in a museum somewhere, not underground, hidden away from the world. She traced her fingers along a carved edge and admired the craftsmanship.

"Guess I'll go first," Thomas said. He bounded up two steps at a time, foregoing the delicate handrails.

"You'll have to excuse Thomas." Lee bowed and motioned Ayla forward. "Ladies first."

Ayla gripped the hand-carved rails and went slower than Thomas, one step at a time. At the top, she found Thomas hunched over a podium-like structure jutting out of the floor in the middle of the room. She stepped onto the raised floor and soaked in her surroundings. The room was the size of a normal bedroom, and on each wall were door-sized metal panels that appeared wildly out of place in the wooden treehouse.

"They're ugly," Thomas said, pointing to one of the doors, "but they do the job."

"What are they for?" Ayla asked.

"Portals," Thomas said matter-of-factly. "That one goes *to* the library," he said, pointing to one of the doors. "The other three go to various lower levels under the central square."

Thomas was busy playing with something on the table, but Ayla stared at the doors leading to the lower levels.

Derek is somewhere in the lower levels.

She noted the doors in her memory in case she'd need them later.

Not long after, Lee's head appeared from the staircase, and he jumped up into the room and dusted off his pant legs.

"I'd love to see the library someday." Ayla wanted to call attention to anything but the doors to the lower levels.

"Well, you're in luck, because that's actually part of our plan," Lee said. "We've been working on it for quite some time. Can you pull up schematics?" he asked Thomas. "Daniel will be here any minute."

"You got it," Thomas replied and smashed buttons on the nearby panel. A few seconds later, screens dropped down out of the ceiling, one right behind Ayla and another in the middle of the room. A series of images flashed on the screens, faster than Ayla could recognize them. Out of her peripheral vision, by the staircase, another face appeared, a face she didn't recognize.

"Daniel!" Lee said, striding over to the entrance and reaching out for a hug.

"Daniel, meet Ayla," Lee said, walking him across the center of the room. "Ayla, this is the group's top scientist, Daniel."

Ayla grabbed and shook his hand, which was warmer than most. He was just as pale as everyone else, but not nearly as worn-down and weary as Thomas. His clothes were in better shape too.

"It's nice to finally meet you," Daniel said with a smile. "You've been the talk of the town lately."

"Thanks . . ." She didn't know what else to say.

Lee stepped in to break the awkward silence. "Like I said, Daniel is the brain for us, and I think he finally has something figured out, right?"

"Right," Daniel said, shifting his gaze from Ayla to the screen in the middle of the room. "The research and development team has been testing bi-directional portals for the past few years. I've been working on my own in secret, just for our group."

He pinched and zoomed on the screen to a section of the library.

"This door here," Daniel said, pointing across the room to one of the doors, "is supposed to be a one-way to the library. That's it. Nothing else. But what I've been working on . . ." He took a couple of steps toward the aforementioned door. "Well, it's probably easier to show you." He pressed a button on the center console. The metal plate on the wall slid away, revealing a red gel-like substance. Without a word, Daniel jumped toward the wall and disappeared.

Thomas and Lee both stared at where Daniel had just disappeared, completely silent. Ayla watched the door, waiting for something to happen, and then something did. Daniel appeared from the same door and landed with a loud *thud* as his feet made contact with the wooden treehouse floor. He paused after landing, like a gymnast doing an Olympic routine, and then, in a dramatic flair, he stuck out his hands.

Lee mouthed the word "whoa" and started clapping enthusiastically.

Thomas put his hands on top of his head and whispered, "It *is* possible . . ."

"Proof of concept is there, but I need your help now in hooking it up to one of the bigger, external portals," Daniel said.

"Wait." Ayla took a step forward. "So, you're going to reverse one of the external portals and escape that way?"

"Bingo," Lee said.

"There's one minor issue though," Daniel said. "There are only three external portals we could realistically use." He scanned the room, catching the eyes of Thomas and Lee. "The one Clay uses is off the list."

Lee nodded in agreement.

"There's the sunlight portal here," Daniel added, "but I can't draw enough power in to make it bi-directional. It's too large."

"I'd prefer to use our own, if possible," Lee said.

"I would too," Daniel said. "Even if I *could* get enough power out here, the amount of attention I'd get just isn't worth it."

Lee sighed.

Daniel continued. "So, I think our only true choice is our last option: the Mirror in the central square." The group remained silent, so he went on. "It's large enough and it already has enough power routed to it, so it meets all of our criteria except for easy access."

"That seems risky," Thomas said. "Having us all run through the central square?"

Lee started pacing. "I don't like it—"

"I think we could mitigate our risks a little," Daniel said. "I've talked to some of our facilities people, and they seem to think they could lower it and make it easier for us to access, at least from the top of the Beacon."

"Still, that doesn't seem . . ."

Ayla let her mind wander as Lee trailed off. She was confused by most of the conversation, anyway, so she didn't think it would hurt to come up with ways to track down and find Derek. If she could get some alone time to jump through one of these lower-level portals, she might be able to find him.

She needed more time by herself.

She needed separation.

She needed to escape again but wasn't sure how.

As everyone in the room kept talking, she weighed the pros and cons.

". . . and it would have to be done in the middle of the night." Daniel turned to Ayla, who was only half-listening. "Do you see any issues with us heading outside when the sunlight disappears?"

"Um . . ." She stalled. "Well, it'll be dark, obviously." She got blank stares from Daniel, Thomas, and Lee. "So . . . so it'll be harder to navigate and orient ourselves." She struggled and searched for more words to add value. "But . . . with what you're talking about trying to do . . . I don't see any better options."

"It sounds like that might be our only choice," Lee said. "The group is gathering by the pond now. I'll make the announcement."

THIRTEEN

Tortured

Derek wasn't able to keep track of anything other than the times food was brought to him. He had eight meals show up in his room so far, and they always appeared when he slept or had nodded off. He assumed they were delivered through the door he still hadn't figured out how to open. After tracing the door, he had come to the conclusion there were letters and numbers engraved on the back. There were three at the top, which he deciphered to be "WW-5."

At the bottom was a mix of numbers and letters he couldn't quite make out. The engravings didn't seem to do much of anything, and between meals, he imagined all sorts of wild scenarios of what they meant. He had also been drawing up ways of how to open the mysterious door or how he could trick it into opening so he could escape.

Before his ninth meal appeared, he lay in bed, pretending to sleep. He watched the door through his eyelashes, waiting for the moment they delivered the food. His skin rubbed against the scratchy sheets, and he wanted nothing more than to reach down and relieve his itch, but he held still. His training reminded him it was all a mental game, and he focused on the red outline of the door and his need to escape.

He didn't know how long he waited, but eventually, the red light appeared at the bottom of the door, and it slowly opened toward the ceiling. The size of the red light grew until it occupied the entire space where the door had once been. Not wanting to blow his cover, he waited for an opportunity.

He opened his eyes farther and got a more clearly defined picture of the door, now a red rectangle of goo. The red liquid-like substance wavered off in the distance. He was now more tempted than ever, but he kept his eyes mostly closed and his itches unscratched.

A disturbance in the liquid material caught him off guard, and from out of nowhere, his meal slid along the bottom, sending ripples through the goo. When his plate came to a stop, he jumped out of bed and lunged for the door. Before he could reach it, the metal sheet slid back into place, crashing into the floor and leaving nothing but the faint red traces of light along its sides.

"Let me out!" Derek pounded on the solid metal door. "Please!" he pleaded, praying it would slide open again and he'd be free. The sounds echoed throughout the tiny cell and left him feeling more hopeless than before. There was no chance they would let that happen again. Derek had missed his only chance of escape.

He grabbed the plate off the ground and threw it across the room. The hard plastic plate smashed into the brick wall, sending rice and beans flying in every direction. The plate landed on the concrete floor, spinning around until it finally dropped to a rest. He plopped down on the bed, which was now partially covered with food, and put his head in his hands. Derek sat in that position until his stomach needed food. He composed himself long enough to gather bits and pieces of the meal off the floor and bed and sat against the wall to eat.

Derek was woken up by two men. They tossed a bag over his head and dragged him down another maze-like hallway he didn't try to memorize this time. A long time had passed since his last meal, and he assumed they stopped feeding him so he couldn't try to escape again. When the bag was removed, Derek found himself in front of Clay, who sat in a chair and stirred a Styrofoam cup of liquid, like the first time they had met.

"Do you know where you are, Derek?" Clay asked without giving Derek much of a chance to react to his new location.

Derek licked his lips and tried to clear his dry throat. He blinked a couple of times and looked around the room. It was the same room as last time.

"No, then?" Clay replied without giving Derek time to respond. "You're underground, Derek. It's under where you and Ayla were trespassing."

Derek wanted to be anywhere but here. He recalled his training and tried to block out his surroundings.

He longed to see Ayla again, to hold her, to be with her.

He missed the smell of her skin after a shower and the way she laughed at stupid old movies.

He missed her sense of adventure.

In his holding cell, he had a lot of time to reflect on his situation, and he had put Ayla's betrayal far behind him. He couldn't hold a grudge down here. Derek just wanted to move on and be with her again.

"Derek?" Clay stomped forward, drink in hand, peering at Derek, who was now daydreaming about his former life. "Derek, look at me." Clay continued his pace. "Derek." His voice echoed off the walls and the clacking of his shoes increased in frequency. "Derek!" Without breaking stride, Clay launched his Styrofoam cup into Derek's lap.

Derek reached forward with his arms, which were still handcuffed, and the pain of the hot liquid snapped him back to attention. His outstretched palms, now covered in hot coffee, had deflected most from his body, but on instinct, they recoiled back into his lap to shield them from the pain.

"Fuck!" Derek screamed. The word burned his dry throat.

"Do I have your attention?" Clay leaned down to eye level with Derek, who sat and writhed in the cold metal chair, a sharp contrast to the hot coffee splattered on his lap. "What the hell were you guys doing exploring our little underground hideout?"

"I swear we didn't know."

"Bullshit."

"I swear."

"Nobody explores old abandoned buildings and happens to find a long-forgotten, hidden entrance to an underground facility."

"How would we have known?"

"That's the million-dollar question, isn't it, Derek? Who are you working with? Is it Richard? Is he trying to get rid of me?"

"I don't know any Richards." Derek tried to wipe his hands on his pants but had to contort his wrists and forearms to work with the handcuffs.

"Someone else then?"

"No. I don't know!"

Clay snapped upright and headed to the side of the room where Derek had spotted a giant door the last time he was here. When he reached the wall, he grabbed the oversized handle, slid it open, and revealed a black nothingness. Derek peered into the darkness, hoping to make out what was beyond, but he saw nothing.

Clay whipped around and picked up one of the remaining chairs at the table. He dragged it across the floor, and a loud squealing sound echoed off the walls. Derek tried to clutch his ears, but his handcuffs didn't spread far enough apart. Clay approached the wall, dragging the chair behind him. When he was three feet away, he turned around and clutched the backrest with both of his hands. In one quick motion, he tossed the chair against the wall.

Derek braced for an impact, but to his amazement, instead of crashing off the wall, the chair sank into the black abyss like a coffee stirrer into dark espresso. For a brief instant, as the chair passed through the wall, the edges lit up in bright white before it sank all the way in and disappeared. Seconds after, the chair was gone, and a warm wind came out of the wall and engulfed the room in hot air, like a nearby fireball. Clay wiped his brow and turned to face Derek.

"What the hell was that?" Derek snapped at full attention. Clay casually strolled his way.

"That's what we call the pit, Derek. Nobody knows where it goes or what's in it. What we throw into the pit never comes back. You don't want to find out for us, do you, Derek?"

It sounded like a question, but Derek knew it wasn't.

"Nobody wants to find out, Derek, so tell me how you found out about this place." Clay's voice grew louder with each word. "You're not supposed to be here!"

"I've already told you what I know." Derek hung his head. He didn't have enough energy to fight back.

"I'm sorry." Derek almost didn't hear Clay's faint voice. "I don't think that's true. And I don't think the pit thinks that's true either." He signaled to one of the security guards standing behind Derek, out of his vision. Clay approached Derek, and all Derek could do was put his hands up in a meaningless show of resistance. The two men effortlessly lifted and carried his chair over to the entrance of the pit. They dropped the chair legs mere inches from the front of the black chasm.

"What do you think, Derek? What do you think is in there?" Clay grasped the partially open door with one hand and Derek's handcuffs with the other. He lifted the handcuffs closer and closer to the wall. Derek let it happen at first, but his instinct took over and he pulled back, hard.

The force from Derek's hands caused Clay to stumble before gripping the door handle tighter and nudging the guard standing behind Derek. The guard's giant hand reached down and joined Clay's in holding Derek's handcuffs. Both men forced Derek's hands forward, and the little resistance Derek could muster made no difference at all.

"What do you think it is, Derek?" Clay shouted, now inches from Derek's face as he and the guard moved his hands toward the abyss. "Tell me if it hurts."

Derek glanced away from the wall and caught a glimpse of

Clay's fiery face, eyes twisted and nostrils flared. Derek closed his eyes and held a deep breath, not knowing what to expect. He braced for the unknown.

He heard metal striking metal, and the very next instant, sharp pain exploded across his knuckles and spread out down to his wrist. On instinct, he pulled his hand back. Both the guard and Clay seemed to have lost their grip, and Derek opened his eyes. He peered down, hand clasped between his legs, to see a mangled mess of fingers protruding in different directions and bloody spots across his knuckles, which were covered in large bruises that slowly engulfed his entire hand.

It didn't take long for his hand to swell and balloon beyond recognition. He glanced upward to Clay's smiling face. He was still holding the handle of the door, which Derek now realized had been slammed on his hand. He hadn't entered the pit at all. On the wall, blood was smeared where his hand had been.

His body was in shock, and up to this point, he hadn't processed how much pain he was actually in. It started at his elbow and crept up his arm to his shoulder and around his back, then finally hit his brain like a freight train. He howled, clutching his hand between his knees, and fell out of his chair and onto the floor.

He curled into the fetal position, sucking air through his clenched teeth. The lights started to dim, and Derek wasn't sure if he was blacking out or not. He felt like he was having an out-of-body experience, and he could almost see himself in third person, lying on the floor.

"He's over here," Derek heard Clay say in the distance.

Between long blinks, Derek realized that Clay was now talking to others in the room. Wearing white masks that covered their faces, they knelt next to Derek on the floor. They tried to pry away his broken hand from his grasp. After struggling for a few seconds, he let them have it. With a few unseen motions, they wrapped his hand in a squishy material, the inside of which felt cool, like a baseball mitt that had been sitting in the freezer.

The pangs in his hand dulled, and he was finally able to slow his breathing. His tunnel vision dissipated, and his out-of-body experience retreated. The two faceless figures stood up and fled the room. Clay still held onto his grimacing smile.

"I wouldn't take that off your hand if I were you." Clay stepped closer. "It will prevent you from losing it."

FOURTEEN

Foresight

Katherine needed a break. Ever since she found out that Ayla had escaped, she had done everything in her power to try and track her down, but she and Jeffrey were having no luck. She was hoping a brisk walk around the central square would help her focus again. When she arrived at the lobby of the hospital wing, she saw the last person she wanted to see.

"Found her yet?" Ellen called out from the lobby door.

"I'm surprised Clay's not with you, knocking down my door." Katherine crossed her arms.

"Oh, he knows." Ellen took a step forward. "I filled him in, and now he wants me to help him track Ayla down, since you seem to be doing an awful job of it."

"She's not here," Katherine said.

"Even if you had found her, you wouldn't tell me."

"She's *not* here." Katherine stood taller.

"If we find out she *is* here, you're not going to want to hang around too long." Ellen took another step closer to Katherine. "We'll be coming for you."

"*We*? Are you and Sam threatening me?"

"Sam?" Ellen scoffed. "No, no, no. *We* meaning me and Clay."

"You're doing his dirty work for him now?"

"Hardly."

"What do you get out of helping him?"

"Everything." She sneered at Katherine.

Katherine hadn't noticed Jeffrey walk up behind her until he spoke. "What seems to be the problem?" he asked.

"Are you helping her conceal the spy?" Ellen directed her question at Jeffrey.

"I'm helping contain the situation," Jeffrey calmly replied.

"Based on the rumor mill and panic levels everywhere, including your own hospital"—she gestured down the hallway, and a nurse dropped her head and walked away from the lobby—"I can see you're doing a *fine* job of it."

"Are you doing much better?"

"I have a starting point." Ellen lifted her chin. "And I'm going to use it." She paced in front of the lobby couch. "The hospital security videos show her leaving here."

"Security videos?" Katherine blurted out. "How'd you get those?"

"Raymond likes me, I guess."

"Did you threaten him?"

"I didn't have to."

Katherine and Jeffrey made eye contact.

Raymond didn't let us see anything.

"What'd you see on the tapes?"

"I'm sure you'll be interested to hear that she left with Thomas."

Jeffrey turned again to Katherine and mouthed, *Thomas?*

"I'm concerned about Thomas's prior alleged associations with that pitiful faction," Ellen said.

"That was a long time ago, Ellen," Jeffrey said. "What use would she be to a group like that?"

"It's not hard to imagine. Let me see . . . a group wanting to escape this place and find out what's above ground. What could they possibly want with someone who claims to be *from* above ground?" The sarcasm dripped out of her mouth.

"A lot of things have changed since then."

"That's what the tape shows, so either Thomas acted alone and kidnapped her for some random reason," Ellen said, "or the faction is alive and well and have her."

"I find both of those hard to believe," Katherine said.

"Either way, I have to flush them out." She headed toward the door but stopped short and turned to face Katherine and Jeffrey. "Unless, of course, you two know something."

Jeffrey shrugged and Katherine ignored the question.

"How are you planning to flush them out?" Katherine asked.

"Lee's predecessor was head of that pointless uprising last time. I think it only makes sense to start there again."

"It's not Lee," Katherine said.

Ellen opened the door and shouted over her shoulder, "Once I have a chance to talk to him, I guess we'll find out."

"It's not Lee!" Katherine cried out again, but the doors had already slammed shut. "It can't be Lee," she said to Jeffrey this time. She threw her hands up in the air. "Lee has nothing to gain from this. It doesn't make sense."

"Why not?" Jeffrey pulled a cigarette from his case.

"It just—it just couldn't be him. I *know* him. He's not like his predecessor. He would never start that group up again."

"I'm not convinced we ever know anybody quite the way we think we do." He stuffed his cigarette in his mouth.

Katherine scratched her head and wandered to the over-stuffed, haggard chairs against the wall and plopped down, sending air rushing out of the bottom. Jeffrey made his way over, his cigarette moving between his mouth and his hand seamlessly. He stood next to Katherine, who dropped her head to her knees.

She ran everything from the past few hours through her mind: the conversations, the actions, the thoughts. They had talked to Raymond, but he was adamant about washing his hands of the situation. Maybe they got to him after Ellen, or maybe Katherine didn't push as hard as Ellen.

She had briefly talked to Lee, but he seemed oblivious to the entire situation and only remembered him telling her he would "keep his eyes out" and "be on guard," but beyond that, he was his normal, lost-in-the-clouds, imaginative self. Katherine found it very difficult to believe he was harboring a fugitive. Her mind always circled back to Ellen.

What had Ellen and Clay talked about?

Katherine didn't expect Clay to delegate most of his duties to Ellen; that didn't seem to be his style. In the past, Clay had taken charge, solved the issue, and carried on with life, more or less, minus a hiccup after the last time.

The last time . . .

The last incident . . .

Nobody wanted another incident . . .

Clay delegating to Ellen . . .

She jerked her head up from between her legs.

"Katherine—" Jeffrey clutched at his chest.

"What did you say?" Katherine asked.

Jeffrey quizzically stared at her.

"Earlier." She stood up. "Something about how we don't think we know people?"

"I believe it was more eloquent than that."

"I *know* Ellen, and I *know* Clay, and I *know* what's happened here." She turned to Jeffrey. "Do you remember what happened *after* the incident?"

"Quite frankly, it was hell."

"Exactly," Katherine continued. "There's no way Clay wants that again. It probably made his life ten times harder. It makes sense, then, why he sent Ellen here. He wants it taken care of quickly and, more importantly, silently. Right?"

"I suppose." Jeffrey took a drag from his cigarette.

"And Ellen is trying to bully people to get her to help. Me, Raymond, whoever else she's pulled into this . . ." She paced in a semicircle around the lobby chairs. Jeffrey didn't move, staring ahead as always. Katherine stopped mid-stride. "But why would she come here to tell me her plan? That's not something Ellen does, right?"

This doesn't make sense.

Ellen never involved Katherine and hardly spoke to her unless she had to. Ellen was a woman on a mission, and regardless of what was in her way, she'd finish it herself. She wanted as little help as possible, maybe every now and then some from Sam, but he would never get too involved. Jeffrey remained silent, sucking on his cigarette, and the swirl of smoke wafted past her nose.

"She knows I'm closer with Lee than anyone, and she would assume we would help each other."

"What do you mean?"

Katherine stood frozen. "I think she came here hoping for a deal."

"A deal?" Jeffrey pushed his glasses up his nose.

"She doesn't know where Ayla is, and for all I know, she's making up that story about Thomas."

Jeffrey puffed his cigarette again.

"If she had to find her, she'd start with asking everyone in the group. She must not have her, and we know she talked to Raymond, who must not have her, so that leaves me and Lee."

"And myself," Jeffrey added.

"Sure," Katherine said.

"Why would the limit just include the five of us?" he asked.

"What better place to start? And Lee can tend to be more . . . inaccessible, I'd say. But she knows where to find me. Or us." Between frantic steps, Katherine verbalized her thoughts. "And she comes to talk to try and flush Ayla out. To try and force a confession, she threatens us with Clay and with Lee."

Jeffrey nodded. "I think I see where you're taking this," he said. "As a pure hypothetical, let's say you *are* hiding Ayla somewhere. Ellen calls you out on it, you deny it, and she threatens to take it to Clay. In this scenario, she's hoping you cave and admit to having Ayla to save your friend Lee."

"But in the real-world scenario where I *don't* have Ayla, she does the same thing to Lee, hoping he caves."

"Right," Jeffrey said.

"But neither of us have her," Katherine said.

"Are you sure about that?"

"She can threaten whoever she wants," Katherine continued, ignoring Jeffrey, "but if she can't back it up, what's the point?"

"Keep in mind though, she *can* back it up. With Clay," Jeffrey said.

"But he doesn't want to get involved unless he absolutely has to. She needs Clay for enforcement, and Clay needs her to keep this whole thing quiet."

Katherine tapped her foot and stared at the ground. She watched out of her peripheral vision as Jeffrey smashed his cigarette butt into the ashtray, extinguishing the last flickers of life and watching the dwindling smoke wind up through the ceiling. "Those seem mutually exclusive," he said. "I don't think you can enforce it without raising a stink."

Katherine's head snapped up from the ground. "Exactly!"

Jeffrey jumped back and grabbed at his chest again.

"They aren't. You can't have one without the other."

"What?" Jeffrey asked.

"Does the Beacon still work?" A smile ran across Katherine's face. She didn't wait for Jeffrey's reply. Instead, she turned on her heel and headed for the door.

The hospital doors flung open on the demands of Katherine's keycard and shut before Jeffrey's words reached her. She was sure he had something to say but she didn't want to hear it. People were packed into the central square at this hour, most having an early start to their evening—grabbing something to eat, running errands, or stopping by the supply kiosks to fill up for the remainder of the week.

Katherine didn't have any normal daily activities on her mind as she followed the main marble path, elbowing past the crowd in her way. Calls of her name flew past her, but she kept going. The crowd thickened as she approached the center of the room, but she kept plowing her way forward, ignoring those around her as she headed toward the Beacon only a short distance away. She was sure she had read everything right. She was sure of the situation now, surer than she had ever been.

"Katherine!"

Another call of her name came from behind her, and she ignored it like the others. She focused on her task: reach the Beacon. It grew taller and the details of the speaker system on top jumped to life as she approached. She tiptoed around some vendors and people in the way, sometimes going off the main path but eventually swaying back on.

"Katherine, wait!"

She didn't stop, but she put her hands out, pressing forward, and looked behind her. Jeffrey's balding head stood out in the crowd, and he waved his hand in the air. She was sure he'd provide another lecture or a philosophical debate about one thing or another, but Katherine wasn't in the mood. For the first time in a while, she had made up her mind.

A few paces away from the Beacon, the crowd started to thin. She stepped back onto the marble surface that ran around the outside of the Beacon, reached for her keycard, and extended it toward the door at the base of the building. At the same time, a hand fell on her shoulder. She swatted it away as she turned around to see Jeffrey's yellow teeth grinning at her.

"Didn't you hear me?" he asked.

She turned and swiped her card, and the door disappeared into the stone wall.

"Katherine?" he asked, grabbing at her shoulder again.

"Not now, Jeffrey." She slapped his hand away, stepping into the room, and Jeffrey followed closely.

"I'm in a bit of a hurry."

"I can see that," Jeffrey said. "What are you doing?"

"I need to send a message." She grabbed the wrought-iron railing and headed up the spiral staircase in the middle of the room. The sound of her shoes against the steps echoed off the stone walls. Jeffrey climbed the stairs right behind her.

She had always given him credit for his persistence, but this time, it was a nuisance, and she tried to outrun the problem by taking the steps two at a time.

"Katherine, please wait. What message? What do you mean?"

"Not now, Jeffrey. Please."

"But you always want to talk. Why are you ignoring me now?"

"We said everything we needed to back at the hospital."

"Did we?" He gasped for air.

A few steps from the top, Katherine jumped into the top room and immediately found the electronic controls, which were a far cry from the modern sets they had in the hospital. It had been a while since she had been up here and had to make any announcements. Her announcements were usually medical-related, like those for outbreaks or new treatments, and being outside of her comfort zone, she felt her hands shake again. She messed with the knobs and dials and flipped a few switches to turn the lights from green to red.

"Katherine," Jeffrey huffed and gasped for air as he reached the top level. "Katherine, what message . . . ?" He took a deep breath and exhaled again. "What are you doing?"

"I have to beat Ellen at her own game. She doesn't want Clay involved, right?" She flipped a few more switches and watched the external lights flicker to life and send a shock wave of pink and red onto the surrounding walls. "I'm going to give him no option." She stepped forward and looked out the window. Most of the people below had stopped in place. Some were holding bags, some stopped mid-bite from their sandwiches, and all of them looked upward at the Beacon. Their faces froze in time, a mixture of awe, wonder, and fear. The noise outside dropped to an uncomfortably quiet level.

"What does that mean?" Jeffrey huffed out.

"I'm going to give Ayla a heads up, and Lee too, if that's who really has her."

"And you're going to cause mass chaos below. Look out there," he said, walking to stand next to her at the window. "It's already happening." He pointed down at the crowds encircling the Beacon.

Katherine stared at Jeffrey. "I know."

Jeffrey pulled Katherine's hand away from the controls. "Katherine, talk to me, please."

"I'm going to do this, and you have to trust me."

"Why?" Jeffrey pleaded. "Why this?"

"I'm calling Ellen's bluff. She *has* to be in charge, so what happens if she's not?"

"You'll alert Clay, and he will be here next. Is that what you want?"

"I don't have a choice."

"You'll have to answer to him if you go through with this."

"I can handle it."

"What if Ayla escapes? What about the rebel faction? What if they all get out?"

"Why is it a big deal if they do?" Katherine asked.

"You'll be responsible. You'll have to take the fall."

"I know . . ." Katherine turned back to the electronic control board.

"Katherine, please think about what you're doing. You're going to set in motion actions that cannot be undone."

"What if the faction is right? What if we're prisoners and there is no war above?" Katherine said.

"What if they're *wrong*?"

"Jeffrey, listen, I know you follow the letter of the law, but can't you see past that?"

"Katherine, I—"

"Can't you see the miserable people down here? So what if a few get out? Maybe there's a war. Maybe there isn't. Do you think it really matters anymore?"

"I can't let you do this."

"Why are you so afraid?" Katherine asked.

"Why are you not content? You have everything you could ever need here. I just don't understand." He had to raise his voice as the crowds below them rumbled.

Below, the floor of the central square had disappeared, swallowed up by masses of people staring up and yelling at the Beacon. Some had started pounding on the door, sending reverberating echoes all the way to the second floor.

"It's not about me," Katherine said.

"You'll ruin what we have."

"Maybe that's not the worst thing." Katherine kept turning dials, and as she turned one in the middle, the speakers on the outside blared to life, sending a high-pitched squeaking noise through the square. Katherine turned the dial back to where it was to make the squeaking stop. When it did, Jeffrey shuffled behind her, and in the next instant, something cold slapped her wrist. Jeffrey spun her around, and in one move, he slapped the other handcuff bracelet to her free wrist.

"I told you that you can't do this, and I just can't sit idly by." He tugged on the middle of the handcuffs, but Katherine pulled away and broke free of his grip. She turned and twisted herself to the center console and smashed the big red button with her palms. The speakers came to life again, and this time, Katherine leaned over and spoke into the microphone.

"Lee, they're coming for you and Ayla—"

Before she could finish, Jeffrey pulled her away. "That was very stupid, Katherine."

FIFTEEN

Escaping Eden

"You know I don't feel comfortable with this, right?" Ayla headed down the staircase, holding onto the railing, calling back to Thomas behind her.

"With what?" Thomas asked.

"This plan." Ayla kept walking. "I don't know where this portal is going to lead. What if it goes right to Clay's house or something? What if we all end up in a worse spot?"

"I don't think that's possible," Thomas said.

"Why?" Ayla asked. "We don't know anything about it."

"Didn't you say it should be fine?"

"I did, but—"

"It *has* to work." Thomas stopped on the last step, an intense focus in his eyes. "We have to get out."

Ayla paused and stared back at him. "You really don't like it here, do you?"

He nodded over to the pond in the distance. "All of us found each other with the sole purpose of trying to get out."

"But why? It seems nice here," Ayla said.

"This is nice, yes, but life in the lower levels, where nearly all of us come from, is terrible. Think of the smallest, most confined space you can. There are no windows, no portals, no sunshine, and it's a constant barrage of more work after more work. It's grinding, it's wearing, and it's all anyone knows. But there *has* to be something better. These people know there *has* to be something better. That's why we're here."

Clustered groups of people surrounded the outer edge of the water while Lee, their leader, stood in the middle of a long pier that nearly reached the center of the pond. Ayla noticed the kids. Most ducked and hid behind their parents, some dangled their feet in the pond, and others weren't paying attention at all and instead played close by.

The reality of the situation hit Ayla. This wasn't a fun game of hide-and-seek for them; it was a matter of life and death. Their parents were risking everything, hope hinging on the outside world being better than what they were facing here. Everyone who stood at the edge of the pond was risking all they had, including their futures, however bleak. They were risking it all for something unknown.

"I really don't think I can do this," Ayla said.

"I promise it'll be fine, Ayla. Most of the work is done anyway, remember?"

Keeping in mind these people wanted to escape, she watched the families playing in the distance. They actively had a choice, unlike so many others. Ayla thought back to her mom, happy and content with life until her diagnosis, when she no longer had a say in the matter. Her mother went downhill quickly and didn't even have a choice.

Ayla didn't have a choice on whether or not her father was in her life. It wasn't fair for Ayla, it wasn't fair for her mom, and it wasn't fair for these people to be trapped in this situation, but at least they had some say in the outcome. Ayla could help them find what they so desperately desired.

Her mind flickered to Derek. He didn't have a choice, either. Ayla could help him too. Everyone seemed to need her, and she wanted to help them all, but she had to decide.

As Thomas and Ayla approached the water, the sound of the whispers grew. At first, it was a few faces turning to watch her, but with each step, more heads turned her way and the whispers turned into murmurs, which sparked discussions. Some people turned but pretended they weren't looking at her. Some people covered their mouths in case she might hear them. Some others used their peripheral vision to try and catch a glimpse.

Person after person, face after face, their reactions were similar: eyes wide, mouth open, frozen. It was an odd, uncomfortable, familiar feeling for Ayla. She was transported back in time, when she and her mother went to the grocery store in their small hometown. They walked through the produce section, trying to find the perfect head of lettuce, and in the reflection of the mirrors in the chillers, Ayla caught stares from strangers.

They walked to the bakery to find a reasonably priced loaf of bread, and Ayla heard whispers behind her back. She and her mother would pick out an affordable half-gallon of milk so they could get through the week, and people pushed their carts out of the way to avoid going near them. It was a time Ayla had hoped to have moved on from, but now, in an unfamiliar setting, she experienced the familiar feeling of not belonging. There was genuine curiosity in the air this time because of a *true* outsider, someone who had been outside of this place. She was still an outsider here, but in a very different way.

"Just in time," Lee's voice called out from the pier. He waved to Ayla and Thomas among a small cluster of ten people on the opposite side of the pond. Lee's call made the crowd around them move away instinctively so the honored guests could be seen near the shore. Thomas waved at everyone, and Ayla half-heartedly did the same, still teetering between the edge of the sandy shore and the grass. "Let me introduce our guest here, who you've heard all about. This is Ayla." Ayla kept waving and smiling. "She's going to be helping us once we get to the outside. She's told me a lot about it, and I'm very excited. You all will not be disappointed."

Ayla dropped her hands to her sides. Lee came across as the weird, quirky leader of a cult, which made her second-guess if she was doing the right thing. She didn't know if he was leading them astray or if her time would be better served finding Derek. Seeing as how nobody else seemed focused on rescuing her boyfriend, her thoughts returned to him. He was in immediate danger, and the people here could wait.

Lee spoke from the pier. "I'm happy to announce the successful testing of our escape plan: a two-way portal passage." The hushed awe from the crowd slowly built into a murmuring roar. Lee waved his hands around, trying to dispel the noise.

Ayla wanted to save everyone, but she knew she couldn't. Finding her boyfriend was her top priority; then she'd return for everyone else. The children who'd gathered around the pond were innocent and unaware. She *had* to return, she told herself. Not just for herself and Lee and Thomas, but for them all. But she had to prioritize, and Derek came first.

"I don't feel very good," she said to Thomas.

Thomas reached out, trying to help.

"I'm going to get some air." She took a step back.

"Okay," Thomas said in a hushed voice. "Let me know if there's anything I can do."

Thomas looked concerned, and his heart and intentions were always in the right place, which made Ayla feel bad for the deception. Lee kept talking from the pier, detailing the escape plan in a very long-winded way. Ayla slipped through the crowd, separating them and distancing herself from the shore.

Lee's speech kept people focused as she wiggled her way to the back row, where nothing stood between her and the treehouse but an open field. She wasn't paying attention to Lee anymore, but without warning, the crowd burst into a loud round of laughter, and she took it as a sign. The crowd was distracted, so she turned and sprinted.

She hadn't run in grass in a long time, and the softness of the ground threw off her stride. Her foot sunk ever so slightly into the dirt, and with the contoured hills, she had a hard time keeping her balance. It felt like she hadn't run or used her muscles in years, but the flat hospital hallway was easier to run on than the grassy hills. She tackled one slope after another, closing in on the treehouse with every stride.

Not much farther.

She sprinted the last few yards and huffed the moment she

reached the stairwell. Slowing her momentum, she grasped the railing and put her foot on the first step. For a brief moment, she paused and looked back, sucking in air. Thomas appeared as a dark outline in the distance. The crowd focused on her now instead of Lee.

They would be following her, and she had to make the most of her time, so she turned again and bounded up the stairs as fast as her weak legs could carry her. She reached the top and closely examined the four doors, trying to remember which ones led to the library and which ones led to the lower levels, where Derek was. Holding her breath, she smashed buttons on the center console until one of the doors opened. She closed her eyes, exhaled, and then jumped through the open door.

Her palms slammed against a chain-link fence as she fell out of the other end of the portal. She jerked backward and her back hit the other side of the portal, which flickered and made a noise like a long piece of string stuck in a vacuum. A stinging pain rose from the bottom of her neck and lodged itself behind her eyeball. She grabbed her head and dropped to her knees, hoping the pain would go away.

After a few agonizing moments, the intense pressure in her head faded, and she took a deep breath. She collected herself and focused on the new territory she found herself in. Standing on a catwalk above a giant complex of pipes, gears, and larger-than-life machinery, she felt like an ant in a factory, looking down from above, surrounded by unfriendly, thunderous noises of churning and whirring. Steam and smoke rose from different spots all along the floor, which she guessed was the size of a football field, but it could have been larger. The other end of the floor was too far away for her to see.

She wrapped her fingers around the aluminum fence. There were other walkways crisscrossed throughout the space, all with a row of lights along the top to lead the way for workers. Letting go of the fence and finding her balance on the narrow walkway, she turned to look at the other side of the portal, which was a red blank slate, sitting there and waiting for another person to pop out. She had to distance herself from whoever else might be coming through from the other side.

Her hand dragged against the fence as she shuffled her feet down the walkway and away from the portal. The machine noises changed the farther she went, but the visuals stayed the same. During some of her urban exploration sessions, she had come across old abandoned machinery, never anything quite to this scale, but it was exciting to see everything up and running instead of rusty and old, shrouded in darkness, waiting for someone to stumble upon it and photograph its once-great glory. Giant vats of liquid were spread throughout the floor, and on occasion, a burst of flames would come from some of the tanks.

She maneuvered through different crossing levels of walkways and finally picked a spot to stop and find her bearings. In the distance, a large shed-like building stuck out next to one of the room's walls. The building was set apart from everything else by its windows and lights. She headed in that direction, finding one more ladder before being able to set foot on the ground-floor level.

She trekked toward the shed, keeping her head on a swivel to make sure nobody was around. Once she reached it, she ducked down so she was lower than the front window, crouched, and peeked through to the inside. There were walls full of control boards and monitors, desks full of papers and folders, and randomly spaced rolling chairs throughout. The room seemed devoid of any people, so staying half-crouched, Ayla headed for the door, opened it, and walked inside.

The inside of the room was much quieter than outside, the only sounds being the gentle humming of monitors and the squeaking of Ayla's shoes against the old tiled floor. The monitors displayed what looked like a map of the entire area, with gridlines and shapes indicating where things were located. A lot of the words on it were gibberish or code of some kind, and Ayla only spotted a few she knew: "geothermal," "wastewater," and "electric." She passed the screens and kept moving down the room.

At the far end of the room was a wall with nothing but a giant double door with a button next to it. With nowhere else to go, she pushed the button. Noises came from behind the wall. Ayla took a step back. The next sound was ungodly screeching and banging, like someone scratching a chalkboard with their nails while falling down the stairs.

Ayla took another step back. She scurried inside a small space underneath a desk in case the noises had alerted someone to her presence. The noises grew louder. Ayla covered her ears. There was a *ding* sound, like an elevator, and the double doors spread open. Ayla peered out from her hiding spot and waited. Nobody came after a few minutes, so she crept to the elevator and stepped in.

She found the elevator buttons on the side panel, but they weren't very helpful: G, H, M, U, and S. The S didn't have a button next to it anymore, only a faded circle where a button used to be. Ayla didn't have time to think, so she jammed her finger into the U button.

The elevator dinged, but the doors stayed open. She pushed

it again, but the elevator didn't change. Ayla moved on to the H button, which seemed to make the elevator happier. The H button stayed illuminated, and the doors slid shut. She wasn't sure how much time she had or if she was headed in the right direction. She just had to move and do something—fast.

Moving was better than not moving, and so far, from what she had seen, it would take months to find Derek, if not years. She didn't have time to think about it and lose hope, because that was all she had anymore. She'd search every room on every floor if she had to. The elevator jolted and clanked upward as she held her breath and clung to hope.

The ride to Level H was jerky, bumpy, and annoyingly long. With Thomas and his group on her heels, her patience was growing thin. The elevator finally clunked to a stop and the doors squeaked open to expose a long, bright-orange hallway. Ayla peeked her head out.

To the left and right were just-as-long and just-as-orange hallways disappearing into darkness and carrying on farther than her eyes could see. The elevator groaned and she stepped out entirely. It wasn't clear what H stood for or where she was, and she now had three paths to choose from, none of which looked at all interesting. She opted to go straight ahead. The path was lit with halogen lights. The orange color seemed odd and obnoxious and especially jarring after she had come from the mechanical and dingy space, but Ayla kept moving forward.

Metal doors sprung up every ten feet or so, with numbers etched into them like a dystopian storage floor or a hotel with endless rooms. Buzzing lights and eerie vibes surrounded her. Goosebumps sprang up on her arms, and a chill went down her back. She slowed her pace and glided down the hall. The feeling of disconcerting loneliness washed over her. She forced her way forward, keeping her goal in mind.

After she had passed a few doors, she came to an opening in the hall and stepped in. She found herself in a small breakroom of some kind. It had dirty and dated linoleum flooring. There was an old beat-up table, and cracked and peeling cabinets hung off the walls.

She stepped in and headed for the cabinets, hoping for a clue or map or anything helpful. All she found in the first upper cabinet was crumpled Styrofoam cups and scratched plastic plates.

The second cabinet had more of the same, along with piles of napkins, both clean and dirty. She reached the last cabinet on the wall when she heard a muffled cough coming from the entryway behind her. She spun around. A little girl no older than five or six stood in the doorframe, her mouth agape and eyes staring wide from between her frayed side ponytails.

Ayla took one step toward the girl. "Sorry, I didn't—"

The girl screamed, turned, and ran off down the hallway.

Ayla ran after her, but by the time she reached the hallway again, the little girl was halfway back to the elevator. The girl stopped at one of the doors and ran in. Ayla kept running after her but stuttered to a halt when a man stepped out of the room. Ayla almost fell forward, catching herself at the last minute.

"Can I help you?" The man thundered down the hallway. The sound of his large strides echoed off the sterile orange walls.

"Sorry," Ayla said, breathing hard. "I think I scared your daughter and I wanted to apologize."

The man squinted at her, his mustache twitched, and then he raised his hand and pointed at Ayla. "Aren't ya that girl from the outside?"

The man slurred his words, making it hard for Ayla to understand. She hesitated, thinking carefully of what to say next. "My name's Ayla, sir."

"Yeah, yeah," he said, slowing his steps. "Ayla. That's what they call ya. You're not supposed to be down here."

He came closer, and his singed mustache and yellow-tinted rotten teeth stuck out from his face, which was smeared with soot and grease, making it appear less pale than the others Ayla had seen. She inched herself backward. "They gave me permission. They said I could come down here."

"By yourself?" The man kept walking toward her.

"I was waiting for . . ." Ayla hesitated, looking for the right name. "Katherine," she finally said.

The man nodded as if he had heard something familiar. He stopped, now a few doors down from Ayla. "Where is she?" he growled.

"Sh-She said she was right behind me. We're meeting down here. She should be on the elevator, I think." Ayla swallowed. Her heart started racing and sweat dripped down her forehead and rolled onto her flushed cheeks. She looked past the man, down the hallway, to the little girl's head poking out of their doorway, her ponytails swinging every time she moved.

"Ya look different than I expected." His gruff voice bounced off the wall.

Ayla had never heard those direct words from anybody, but she knew they were the same words behind everyone who went out of their way to avoid her and her mother at the grocery store in her small town. Hearing them spoken directly and bluntly rather than from behind sneers and peering eyes was an odd sensation.

"What'd you expect?"

The man shrugged his giant shoulders. "Your skin is"—he looked up at the ceiling as he searched for the right word—"darker than I thought it'd be." He took another step forward, and Ayla took one back. "How's the outside?" He leaned in and his eyes widened, similar to the look his daughter was giving her from beyond the doorframe down the hall.

Ayla avoided eye contact, wanting to not get into a deep conversation with anyone, let alone this complete stranger nearly twice her size. Beyond the man, at the end of the hall, the elevator lit up. It dinged, and she took the opportunity.

"Oh, look, it's Katherine." She pointed down the hall, past the man, and as expected, he turned to confirm.

Ayla seized the moment and sprinted toward the far end of the hall opposite the elevator, away from the man and his accusations. She didn't care who was actually in the elevator, and she didn't care about saving Derek right now. If she was trapped herself, she couldn't save anyone. The man yelled something, but she didn't hear it. She pumped her legs, and as she ran by doors, she heard some of them opening, but she didn't once dare turn around or peek.

Sprinting and flailing and pounding the floor, her legs felt like they'd fly off at any moment.

She reached the other end of the hallway, smashed her hands against the wall, and turned right on instinct. Another breakroom was a few short sprints away, and when she reached it, she shuffled herself into a corner, underneath a table, and waited.

Ayla panted underneath the table. She pulled up her shirt and tried to muffle the noise. Her body shivered and shook, and she tried not to disturb the dirty tablecloth she used for cover. She folded her knees to her chest and crossed her arms.

At first, the large man flew by the kitchen, but then he reappeared in the breakroom doorframe and scanned the space. His heavy breath carried itself through the room. Ayla heard him head for the lower cabinets and start tearing through them one by one. Before he reached her corner, another man entered the kitchen, and the first mustached man turned around to address him.

"She went down the east wing," the second man said in the same slurred speech as the first.

The first man stood up. "Where do ya want me to go?" he asked.

"I'll look through Room 100 and ya cover the rest?"

The sound of the men's boots carried toward the entryway.

"I told Raymond too," the second man continued. "Best prepare for a lockdown."

"Probably. Meet back at your place?"

"No," the first man replied quickly. "Elevator, just in case."

"Okay."

Both men headed out the door.

Lockdown?

She must have come across as more dangerous than she realized. The name "Raymond" didn't sound familiar, but she hoped he'd be forgiving to someone who was trying to rescue her boyfriend. Either way, she didn't have any true allies down here, and she had to figure out what to do next.

She had blown perhaps her only shot at finding Derek, saving everyone back at the pond, and maybe even escaping at all. Her internal clock ticked faster now, and she had to think quickly.

Traversing her memory and re-tracing what she had seen down here only brought up endless hallways full of doors, but not much else: no false ceilings, no stairwells, no doors without numbers indicating a different type of room.

Are there bathrooms?

She couldn't even remember that. Her options were limited, but staying hunkered down in the corner wouldn't get her any closer to escaping. She controlled her breathing and fought her weak knees enough to stand up. At the entryway, she poked out her head. Not seeing anyone in the hallway, she stepped out.

The two men went into the east wing, so based on pure instinct and nothing else, she headed down what she thought was the west wing. After several doors, she found one without numbers and tried the knob with no luck, so she kept moving. She came upon another numberless door and tried to open it again but failed the same way.

I wonder what's behind these.

She looked up and down both ends of the hall and started kicking the door, hoping it would give way or give up and let her in. Her kick bounced off the walls, and she double-checked that the coast was clear. She kicked it again, and when neither kick let her in and her foot hurt, she gave up. She banged on it with her hands and a door down the hall opened up. An old man stuck his head out, looked up and down the hallway, glossed over Ayla, who was now clinging to the wall, and ducked back inside.

Ayla let out the breath she had been holding and jogged down the hall. The hallway was an endless sight of door after door and room after room. Tired from running, she paused and leaned against another numberless door to catch her breath and take a short break.

Her mind raced back to the trapdoor above ground and how she had been stopped before by a door that wouldn't open. She thought there might be a connection here, except these doors had knobs and the other one didn't. There also weren't any weird markings on this door. She remembered jamming her crowbar into the bottom of the strange WW-8 door to open it, and she wondered if the same thing would work here. Her train of thought was broken by a voice shouting from down the hallway.

"Ayla, stop!"

Ayla froze. She turned to find a man jogging toward her. It wasn't the same man as before. This man was much smaller and sounded less intimidating and weaker, with less of an accent, but she still wasn't going to take her chances. "Stop!" he said again.

She spun around and ran.

"No, Ayla!"

She kept running and didn't turn back. The man's footsteps picked up speed behind her. She found her legs pumping again and her breath struggled to keep pace. He was gaining on her, and her feet became heavier with each step. She bounced down another hallway offshoot and hurled herself forward.

Up ahead, a meager-looking pale face popped out of a doorway. The woman's eyes lit up, and she made hand signals and motioned for Ayla to come inside. Ayla was about ten doors away and didn't like the chances of turning around to face her attacker, but she wasn't sure she could trust a strange woman in a strange place.

Still, she liked her chances better with the strange, welcoming woman than with the man trying to hunt her down, so she slowed, reached out to the woman's open door, and grabbed the frame.

The woman grabbed Ayla's shoulders and pulled her in while at the same time slamming a button against the wall and sending the door downward, where it sealed against the floor.

Ayla and the woman had fallen side by side in the tiny room, and the woman held a finger to her mouth. The two women were sprawled out on the floor—in silence—and waited for the sound of stomping boots to come through the hallway. A few moments after their fall, they heard thumping outside the closed door. The sound grew louder and then faded into the distance. When Ayla couldn't hear the man running down the hallway anymore, she turned to the helpful woman.

"Thank you," Ayla said under her heavy, panting breaths. "Who are you?"

From her pocket, the woman pulled out a small notebook and a stump of a pencil. She scrawled on an empty page and held it up. The note read, *I can help you.*

"Can you talk?"

The woman shook her head.

"I'm sorry . . ." In a place with advanced technology, Ayla was surprised this woman was relegated to using a piece of paper and pencil to communicate.

She looked around the tiny room, and the picture became clearer. The room was barely larger than a prison cell, with a cot in the corner, a toilet behind a semi-open door on the opposite side, a burner, and some kitchen supplies on another wall. Not much else. A small lamp in the corner by the cot provided just enough dim lighting to see your hand in front of your face. There was no orange paint on these walls, just gray, dull concrete. This woman seemed to have drawn the short straw in picking living quarters, unless all the endless rooms here were the same.

Ayla focused back on the communication challenge. There had to be a better way. She recalled having to use some sign language when her brother was younger, but most of what she knew was related to food or diapers. "Do you know sign language?" she asked.

Shrugging, the woman turned back to her notebook and scribbled more. When she held it up for Ayla, the first words were crossed off, and below it were the words *I believe you and the others.*

"The others?" Ayla propped her knees up and pondered. "The others here who are trying to escape?"

The woman nodded.

"Why aren't you with them?" she asked. "In their special place, helping them plan?"

More shrugging.

This would be a tough conversation.

"Do you live here?" Ayla asked.

The woman nodded.

"By yourself?"

Her nod continued.

"What do you do here?"

Holding out one hand flat, the woman took her other hand and pretended to grab something from her palm and put it into the air. She repeated this several times.

"You . . . stock shelves?" Ayla guessed.

The woman nodded enthusiastically.

"That makes sense. You can still see."

Ayla had never seen such a dramatic eye roll.

"I know, I know, stupid. Never mind . . ." Ayla said. "Can you help me get out of here?"

The woman shook her head and shrugged.

"You don't know how to get out of here?"

Thumbs-up.

"Can I stay here until I have a plan?"

The woman's other thumb shot into the air.

Ayla put her own thumb up. It seemed like she might at least have one person here who wasn't trying to chase her down.

SIXTEEN

Next in Line

E llen flipped a switch next to the oversized portrait window in her office to partially open it, letting the commotion from the central square stream in from beneath her. At first, it didn't seem like much: people running to and from the Beacon, some crowding on one side, some on another. She stepped forward for a better look.

She didn't remember any upcoming announcements, certainly not by anybody from her staff, so she wasn't sure why the crowd had gathered around the Beacon. While it wasn't unusual to hear announcements she hadn't been aware of, the typical process included bringing in the leaders for a debrief before any statements were made. She sipped freshly made tea and waited as the crowds below grew larger and more excitable. Some people pounded on the Beacon door, a behavior that raised Ellen's eyebrow.

Ellen dropped her spoon when a high-pitched squeal shot out of the amplification system. The sound quickly stopped, but Ellen slammed her saucer and cup down and picked up her walkie-talkie to message Sam.

"What the hell is going on, Sam?" She tapped her foot as she waited for Sam to come through the other side.

"What do you mean?" Sam's voice crackled through the old technology.

She groaned. "Where *are* you?"

"I'm in the housing level." There was static and a brief pause. "We've tracked Ayla here."

"Things are unraveling up here."

"Keep your meter on," Sam said. "I think we have a good lead."

Ellen slammed her walkie on the table and picked up her cup, closing her eyes and taking a deep breath. After talking with Clay, she had more stress than usual, knowing there was a lot more at stake this time around. If she didn't bring in Ayla, she couldn't imagine what Clay would do. He was unpredictable, and not knowing what was next in the plan made Ellen uncomfortable.

If she wasn't in control, she didn't want anyone else to be, and unfortunately, Clay was always in control, something she had known when they made their deal years ago. She was indentured to him, and he always had the upper hand. He was using her now, a position she hated being in. She had done everything she could to push Katherine to give up Ayla, but Katherine hadn't budged. Her hope now rested with tracking Lee down and convincing him to hand over the spy.

She took another sip of tea between sighs.

The speaker from the Beacon sprang to life again, but only for a moment. The squeaking died down, and a familiar voice came out from the system. Ellen recognized it immediately.

"Lee, they're coming for you and Ayla—" The speakers cut out.

Ellen's teacup shattered against the table.

It was Katherine.

Of all the outcomes Ellen had analyzed, this wasn't one of them. She thought she had all the edge cases covered, but she never envisioned Katherine having the guts to bring this to the public. Clay had all-seeing eyes and ears and would undoubtedly hear of the message, which meant Katherine's life was in jeopardy. Katherine was risking her own life for Ayla's, a move that didn't make sense, a move with unimaginable consequences. Ellen had failed Clay, and now there was panic. Panic was what Clay had wanted to avoid.

She picked up the meter from the table and smashed the communication button. "Sam, we have a problem. Get up here!" She threw the device against the far wall and watched it break into pieces and fall to the floor.

Her attention turned back to the window and the crowds below. How long did she have?

At her desk, she pulled out drawers and threw papers around. She almost broke a nail grasping at the pull-tabs of her drawers, and the only thing that interrupted her intensely focused concentration was a buzzing noise from the far wall. The noise buzzed again, and this time, Sam's voice followed. "Ellen, pick up. Are you there?"

Ellen scurried over to pick up the remaining working pieces of her broken meter. "Tell me you got her."

There was an uncomfortable silence.

"I had her in sight but—"

"You *lost* her again!" Ellen dropped what was left of the device and fell to her knees.

"She turned a corner, and I can't—"

It was happening.

The worst was happening.

She saw her career crumble before her. Possibly her life.

The fire raged, and she could practically see Clay staring her down with his lifeless eyes, berating her for failing, and ultimately throwing her in the pit, a place she never imagined she would be when she stepped into this role. She had *never* failed, and she started to play through the newly formed worst-case scenarios in her head, every one of them ending with her in the pit or something worse, though she couldn't fathom what that was at the moment.

She hung her head in her hands.

The silence was broken again. "Ellen?" Sam's voice echoed through the pieces of plastic and metal on the floor.

Ellen took a deep breath. Wallowing in self-pity wouldn't fix this moment or save her. She collected herself and picked up the pieces of her communication device. "I need you back in my office."

"Do you want me to search—"

"Have someone else do it!" she screamed. "I need you up here."

"Got it."

The line went dead.

How could this happen?

Ellen clamored back to her drawers. Papers flew over her shoulders and rained down on her office floor.

Where did I leave it?

Her memory failed her. She jogged over to the bookshelf, leaving her drawers and cabinets open and askew. In front of a book titled *Planning for the Future and Beyond,* she waved her access badge.

The only people with access to the safe were outside security and the head of technology and research. Seeing as how Clay had never stepped foot in her office, she safely assumed nobody was aware of the contents, or even the placement, of her safe. A square section of the bookshelf sucked backward and slid to the side, revealing a steel plate with a spinning number combination lock. Ellen entered the number she put in when she took over the position, and with a couple of clicking sounds, the steel plate slid down into the wall, revealing the contents of the safe tucked away behind it.

Inside were rare items and supplies that Ellen had stashed away in case of emergency, but she wasn't interested in anything except for the sealed envelope sitting underneath it all. Coins and papers tumbled to the floor as she pulled the envelope out. Turning the envelope over, she confirmed that the three-ring "AURA" seal across the back was still intact. She held the envelope close to her chest and closed her eyes.

Was this the right time to use it?

Was there another option she had overlooked?

She remembered when she came into possession of the envelope. Clay had overtaken most of the facility, and Ellen's predecessor had called her into his office.

"Sit down," he said. "I think my time here is limited." He sighed.

"Don't say that," Ellen said, playing nice. Michael wasn't going to be here longer than two or three hours, tops.

"Stop," he said. "There's nothing to be done now."

"But you've made so much progress here . . ." Ellen had mastered feeding his ego.

"It's not enough. I didn't pay attention to the people and situations around me. I didn't play the game, and now I'm paying the price." He looked her squarely in the eyes. "I don't want you to make the same mistakes I did. I'm respected and people turn to me for answers, sure, but when it mattered, I wasn't there for them. I didn't pay attention to them. I didn't think they mattered." Breaking eye contact, he turned his gaze to the window. "Funny now that they're my ultimate demise."

"I don't know what we'll do without you," Ellen lied.

"I'm sure Clay will lean on you to help with rebuilding whatever it is he decides to leave behind."

"Sir?"

"He needs someone to trust." He paced around his desk. "He no longer trusts me, so you need to take on that role. You will undoubtedly take on my position and help the facility move on from this . . . split."

"Thanks." Ellen knew it didn't matter. She had already been trying to decide if she wanted a new desk or not.

"But you have to know there is something that's been passed down from the very beginning. Every predecessor of mine has had it, and I want you to have it as well." He reached into the top drawer of his desk and pulled out a letter-sized, white, plain-looking envelope. It was sealed with red wax across the back, stamped with the AURA logo. He slid it across the desk to Ellen. It read, "Emergency Evacuation."

"What is it?" she asked.

"A situational plan, I'm sure."

"Shouldn't we use this now?"

"My instincts tell me that it's not the right time."

"How do you know?"

"I don't," Michael said, "but I have to trust my gut. It's gotten me this far." He looked down to the central square, to Clay and the security forces rounding up people below. "Which I guess may not be a good thing . . ."

"How will I know when to use it?"

He simply smiled back at her. "I think you're asking the wrong person."

Ellen read the words again. She had pondered their meaning for a long time. That day stuck with her very clearly. It was the last time she'd seen Michael. The last day she was an apprentice instead of the head of technology and research. The last day she was blissfully unaware of everything Michael had shielded her from. And it was her last day of being free from Clay's full control.

There were no other options, she determined. She was in a jam, and her gut was telling her this was the only way out. She feared she'd suffer the same fate as her predecessor and so many like him that day, and it was something she wasn't ready for. Closing her eyes, she took a deep breath, slid her finger behind the wax seal, busted it down the middle, and pulled out the fragile typewritten note.

To the Head of Technology and Research,

When we initially devised the AURA Operation, we recognized that a situation may arise that requires immediate and urgent evacuation of the facilities. In reading this letter, it is assumed that your current facility is under such a circumstance. Outlined below are the steps to escape and lead you to safety.

SEVENTEEN

Escalated Situation

Derek didn't remember how he got here, his vision was blurry, and he had a difficult time focusing on the face in front of him. His hands were tied together, behind a chair, and he felt a searing-cool pain in one of them. The pain in his hand jump-started his brain, and the blurry face in front of him turned into Clay.

"Welcome back," Clay said, standing in front of Derek. "You look like shit." A smirk ran across Clay's pale face. "So, how have you been?" He walked a circle around Derek's mostly lifeless body.

Derek struggled to sit up in the chair, his weakened muscles and empty stomach groaning in pain.

"I've been good, thanks for asking." Clay didn't wait for Derek to respond, stopped walking, and knelt in front of Derek. "You're going to have to be a lot more talkative than this if you want to get out of here with your other hand outside of a glove." He lightly slapped Derek's cheek twice, stood, and started pacing again, this time walking over to the table and grabbing a piece of paper off it. He headed back to Derek's chair and dropped the paper in his lap. "Do you recognize her?"

"Ayla . . ." The weakness of Derek's voice trailed off into the room.

"Very good!" Clay said, in contrast to Derek's whisper. "And do you know what she's doing here?" Clay's finger slammed down onto the photo and pointed to Ayla next to another man in a hallway.

Derek didn't recognize the location or the other face in the picture. "Walking?" he whispered. The blood dripping from his mouth stung his cracked lips.

"Very funny, Derek. Let me spell it out for you: she's sneaking around our complex. This picture was taken from a security camera in another wing. Now, why would she be doing that? What is she going after?"

"How do I know it's real?" Derek asked.

Clay's eyes widened. "You have two options: you can either believe me or call me out as a liar. In your situation, I know what I would choose." He crouched down again to stare into Derek's eyes. "Now tell me, are you calling me a liar?"

Clay's heartless blue eyes reflected no emotion, not even aggression, just a bare window into his brain. Derek had seen it before, in the military. He wanted nothing more now than to challenge the man in front of him, to stand up and beat him senseless and send him flying into the mysterious pit.

Derek's heart started racing, and he gritted his teeth. No other muscle group cooperated with him, and his energy drained from his body. He didn't have the option to challenge Clay now. "I-I know you're not a liar," he eked out.

Clay broke eye contact and looked behind Derek, presumably

at one of the guards. "Look at that. He does learn." Clay paced in front of Derek this time, stepping in and out of Derek's frame of view. "Let me ask you again. Do you know what Ayla might be doing sneaking around? Is she looking for something? Or perhaps some*one*?"

"I don't know. I don't . . ." Derek paused, closed his eyes, and took a deep breath.

He tried flexing his stomach muscles to send blood flowing to his brain.

He had to clear his head.

He had to do something, *anything*.

A shock of adrenaline ran through his body as he exhaled, followed by a twinge of energy. "I don't know anything about this place. *She*," Derek emphasized, "doesn't know anything about this place." He caught Clay's eyes again. "I don't know who you are or what you want." Derek inhaled again, and the air helped clear his mind. His energy was slowly coming back.

Clay slammed his polished shoe into the ground and turned to face Derek. "And I told you I don't believe that for a second." He knelt again over Derek. "I'm going to do what I need to do to protect this place, and I'm especially not going to let some dumb brute and his bitch girlfriend ruin it."

Derek's vision tunneled in on Clay's face. Everything else in the room became blurry. He used every last ounce of focus and energy he had to jerk his head forward. His forehead connected with Clay's, and Clay stumbled and fell backward. Derek smiled. It hurt, but it was worth it. The satisfaction, however, was short-lived. A sudden stinging pain shocked the back of Derek's head. Out of his peripheral vision, Clay scrambled back to his feet, holding the cut on his head.

"You think you're clever?" Clay asked, wiping blood from his forehead. He flung open the sliding door, revealing the empty blackness of the pit. "Remember your old friend here? Did you miss it so much you had to see it one last time?" He stepped over to Derek and kicked him in the gut. The chair fell back, but it was caught by the guards. "As I toss you inside, call out and let me know what's in there. I'd love to know."

Derek levitated in the air as the guards behind him picked up the chair. They managed to move him a couple of feet closer to the pit before another person came running into the room.

"I think we have a problem," the new voice said.

"Can't it wait?" Clay spat out the words.

"Someone just sent out a new message from the Beacon about Ayla."

"What?" Clay yelled.

Derek's chair smacked into the floor, and he lost his balance. Neither the guards nor Clay seemed to notice or care when Derek tipped over backward. His full weight slammed directly on top of his hand. Derek let out a guttural scream.

Clay kicked him. "Shut up," he said.

The pain was like nothing Derek had experienced before, and while the initial shock of slamming into the floor was excruciating, the pain subsided as he turned his focus to Ayla. Whoever gave Clay the news had also informed Derek that this was no joke and Ayla was safe somewhere, presumably down here with him. It was the most relief he had felt in his life. He wasn't sure he would ever see her again, but just knowing she was alive made him feel like he wasn't getting tortured.

My tough girl.

He smiled through his pain, knowing Ayla was safe. Realizing he had been the one getting in her way, he felt a twang of guilt. If he would have been more open to her reckless adventure-seeking ways, this situation could have been avoided. Her grit and tenacity were what he admired about her. He started to think he had taken her for granted.

His muscles instinctively flexed as another shot of pain ran through his hand, up his arm, and hit his brain. Even with the pain, even with the suffering, the feeling of knowing Ayla was out there, safe and cunning as always, gave him hope. He couldn't sit around anymore. He had to give more. He had to remind himself of the reason for continuing through the pain and suffering.

The pain shot out through his body again, and he squeezed his eyes closed and drowned out all the sounds around him. He tried to remember the good times with Ayla and Bella, the good times on the outside. When he opened his eyes again, Clay stood above him.

"You're going to finally help me out, Derek." Clay's face leaned in and Derek caught sight of his wound, redder now and smeared with blood. Clay grabbed him by the back of the shirt collar and forced him to his feet and across the room. Derek winced with each step as the two walked closer to an open door at the back of the room. Derek had never been outside of this room or his holding cell without a hood over his head. He was surprised to see it was a sterile hallway with three other interrogation rooms. He wondered if they all had a pit behind one of their walls or if his was the only one.

They passed the rooms and came to the end of the hallway. Derek didn't see anywhere else to go, no doors or other means of an exit, but the guards kept approaching the dead end. When one guard nearly ran into the wall, he tapped a card against a panel off to the side.

One of the guards kicked the metal. "Not working again, Clay," he said.

"Jam something in it. We need to get up there!" Clay shouted.

The guard reached out for the bottom of the wall with something in his hand that Derek couldn't see. The guard jiggled it around, and then the wall shot up and disappeared, leaving behind the same goo-like substance Derek had seen before. Without hesitation, the first guard jumped into the wall and disappeared. Derek squinted ahead and was positive he was hallucinating until the second guard did the same. A small ripple shuddered through the weird wall, stopping at the frame of the door. Clay pushed Derek ahead of him.

"Don't worry, I promise this one is easier than the pit. Go on." He nudged Derek in the back, and Derek lurched forward. He stopped inches from the warping wall, stuck his foot partially through, and it disappeared. He pulled it back and inspected it.

"Come on!" Clay shouted from behind Derek, kicking him squarely in the butt, sending him headfirst into the wall. Derek landed on the other side and was surprised to find a face full of dirt. Without time to think, he was dragged to his feet and stood up by the guards grasping his armpits.

A weird cooling sensation lingered throughout his tingling body, and he involuntarily shivered and let out a groan.

"You get used to it," one of the guards said.

"Let's go," Clay said, appearing behind them and striding forward.

The guards marched Derek in silence down the dimly lit hallway lined with orange- and red-tinted light bulbs every few feet. A
few hallways veered off the main one they followed, but they were
somehow more poorly lit, and Derek couldn't see what was down
them. Before long, they came to an elevator and one of the guards
swiped the same card as before. A white indicator light came on
above the elevator doors. Derek heard rumbling from above, and
the walls and floor started to shake. The doors opened, revealing
a brightly lit elevator.

"All aboard. Come on," Clay said, kicking Derek in the
back again.

Derek lurched forward, the guards at his sides still holding his
arms. They all entered the elevator, and one of the guards reached
out and punched the button with the letter G on it. The doors
slammed shut and Derek winced at the noise. The guards tightened their grip on his arms.

The elevator groaned and staggered upward, sending Derek
stumbling around the cramped space. They passed floors labeled
U and M, then another floor, and an agonizingly long, bumpy ride
later, they passed H. Eventually, the old, slow elevator reached its
destination and the letter G was outlined in a white glow.

Clay pulled out a pistol from the holster tucked inside his
jacket, briefly inspected it, and pointed it at the door.

The doors opened, and the guards rushed Derek outside. The
room opened up and turned into a giant, cavernous area. Derek's
attention immediately jumped to a skinny building not too far off in
the center of the room. At the base was a large gathering of people
looking up and staring at something Derek couldn't see. His attention was pulled in different ways as the guards walked him forward.

The few people who weren't by the center room scattered away from the group, some ducking behind chairs and others running in the opposite direction. Clay brandished his weapon and waved it in the air. Those in the center of the room turned their focus in his direction and screamed. Mothers grabbed the hands of their children, people dropped their food wherever they were and took off, and some panicked and dropped straight to the floor. Once-occupied chairs tipped over as everyone scrambled out of the way as fast as they could.

A giant round mirror hovered above them and streamed in bursts of light. Against the walls were walkways where other people had stopped and crouched below the railings, while others leaned over to catch a glimpse of the source of the noise on the first floor.

Clay pointed his gun straight up and let off a shot. The noise bounced around the hall and induced more screams, followed by echoes of silence.

"Now that I have your attention," he said, raising his voice so those on the upper stories and walkways could hear him, "if one of you could point me to where I could find Ayla, the outsider, I would greatly appreciate it." Clay's gun clicked, and a cold pressure jammed against the back of Derek's head. "And if I don't see her in thirty minutes, I'm blowing her boyfriend away."

EIGHTEEN

Newfound Ally

Ayla thought it was ironic that the only person who was willing to listen to her was someone who couldn't talk back. It was a nice change of pace from people like Katherine and Lee, who seemed to push their own agendas on her.

While plotting a rescue attempt for Derek, Ayla had learned a lot about her newfound roommate. Over conversations, she found out that the woman's name was Shirley, and she had been mute her entire life due to trauma during birth. Growing up, she was shunned by the community, but they found a spot for her working in the lower levels, mostly because they could use all the help they could get. She primarily stocked shelves, which kept her busy, but it was not terribly rewarding work.

"I understand how that goes," Ayla would say, thinking back to her bartending and waitressing jobs, which now seemed like a lifetime ago. She wondered if those jobs would be waiting for her whenever she escaped.

As great as it would be not to have to work, she wasn't in a position to lose her jobs. It wasn't her top concern now, but it lingered in her mind. She had taken a piece of paper of her own and tried to diagram her location, with Shirley's help of course, but it was slow going, and she quickly found that Shirley didn't know much, if anything at all, about Clay and security. She had heard of them, assuming Ayla interpreted the hand motions correctly, but never saw or interacted with them in any way.

"Do you know where they might be keeping Derek?" she asked.

Shirley shook her head.

"I had heard it was down here somewhere in the lower levels." Looking around the room, Ayla asked, "Is there anywhere down here where nobody goes or somewhere they could hide prisoners?"

Shirley scribbled and held up paper: *Supply room?*

"I might have been there. I don't know," Ayla said. "There were a lot of machines."

Shirley shook her head.

"I didn't see anything that looks like a prison."

Shirley shrugged.

Ayla jumped at a sound behind her and turned to see what it was. Mounted on one of the walls was a display screen that had scrolling text, accompanied by matching audio coming from a hidden speaker.

A scripted, robotic voice boomed through the small room. "An incoming announcement from the central square." There was a pause before the message continued in a different, familiar voice. "Lee, they're coming for you and Ayla." The recording stopped, and the first robotic, feminine voice chimed in. "That is all. Thank you." The audio stopped, the scrolling text went blank, and Ayla sat in horror.

The human voice belonged to Katherine, Ayla was sure, but it made her even more confused.

How did she know I had been with Lee?

Katherine sounded panicked too, like she was in danger, and although Ayla knew the situation would escalate once she escaped and raised alarm bells, she didn't want to cause anyone else harm. After all, everyone down here seemed miserable and trapped, and the last thing she wanted to do was to put them in more danger than they already were. She couldn't imagine the little girl with the pigtails being on lockdown because Ayla was running around or someone like Shirley being confused as to why they were being treated worse than normal.

Ayla turned to Shirley. "Can you play that again?"

Shirley nodded. She flipped a switch on the wall, and the message played again. Ayla confirmed her suspicions: the voice came from a panicked Katherine.

"Where's that coming from? What's the central square?" she asked.

Shirley pointed upward, then, on her paper, scribbled something and held it up: *It's a big room above us.*

Ayla wasn't sure which way was up sometimes. Pausing and taking a deep breath, she collected her thoughts. She couldn't give up on her hunt for Derek but started to think that aimlessly wandering around these levels wasn't the best plan; she'd either get herself killed or attacked or make life even worse for the people trying to live out their innocent lives. She reflected on the group she had run away from at the pond.

If Katherine tried to warn Lee, surely he and his group were in more danger than before. If Katherine knew, and this announcement was broadcast everywhere, then Clay and everyone else knew. She had jeopardized Lee's entire struggle to escape, and she couldn't live with herself on that point. She'd have to temporarily pause looking for Derek and make sure she hadn't inadvertently made things worse for everyone else trying to escape.

If she had to sacrifice the one for the many, so be it, even if the one was the man she wanted to spend the rest of her life with. She thought about the possibility of bargaining with those searching for her, and maybe they'd let Derek go. The possibilities continued to swirl in her head until she paused again and focused on the task at hand. She took in another deep breath.

"Can you get me there?" she asked, standing up and brushing off her pants.

Shirley nodded.

Ayla leaned down to face Shirley, who was a bit shorter than her, and grabbed her by the shoulders. "I don't know what's going to happen, but I'm going to help you. We're going to get out of here, okay?"

Shirley nodded again.

They embraced, and the message repeated itself. The concern inside of Ayla grew. Something wasn't right. Everything that had gone wrong was her fault, and she was the only one who could fix it. She let go of Shirley and stood back up.

"Let's get out of here."

NINETEEN

Rescue Mission

Shirley leaned out the front door and surveyed the hall. Ayla followed her, and when the coast was clear, they snuck out and crept down the hallway at a careful pace, passing descending-numbered doors. They reached the end of the hall and turned right at door twenty. The familiar elevator doors appeared off to the left-hand side, within spitting distance.

Ayla patted Shirley on the back, and when Shirley turned around, Ayla gave her a thumbs-up. Shirley smiled. They got closer and closer to the elevator, and when they were within feet, the doors opened and hordes of people poured out. Ayla made herself skinny against the wall, and Shirley stood in front of her to hide her from those in the crowd, but they didn't seem to care about Ayla or Shirley. They were all focused on where they were heading, whispering among themselves.

Their faces looked as if they had seen a ghost or something equally frightening. Parents coddled their children, and families huddled together. Everyone scurried around and out of the elevator. Ayla and Shirley slipped past them with ease, and once inside, the doors closed and Shirley punched the G button.

"Central square?" Ayla asked.

Shirley held a thumb up.

The old elevator rumbled and clanked and climbed upward.

Why even have elevators?

Teleportation seemed like a much better means of transportation here, with minimal side effects, except perhaps the headaches Ayla had been having, which seemed like a minor inconvenience in comparison. She didn't have much time to dwell on the thought as the elevator came to a halt and the doors creaked open.

A swath of people, similarly shocked as those before, waited to get on, so Shirley and Ayla stepped out quickly to let them through. These people, like those in the crowd earlier, tried to avoid eye contact and seemed to not even realize the two women were there; their eyes were directed at the floor, and they whispered things Ayla couldn't hear. She didn't mind not being noticed, and with Shirley in front of her, they crept along the walls and ducked behind a couch off to the side of a wood-lined walkway.

Ayla stepped into a giant, open-spaced room. A beautiful chandelier hung above, beaming in sunlight, sending sparkles of light dancing around the walkways above, and smattering the floor with colorful crystals. A tall circular tower jutted out of the center of the room like an old castle spire. Ayla wanted to stop and take it all in. She instinctively tugged at her shirt, forgetting her camera bag wasn't thrown on her shoulder. Shirley pulled Ayla forward, and the noises in the center of the room drew Ayla's attention. There seemed to be two men arguing, with a few others surrounding them.

Trash was strewn about the ground, and the two of them could hardly walk two feet without having to maneuver around something. As they kept moving, Ayla did her best to remain quiet, and the picture playing out in the middle of the room came into focus. She could make out Lee and another man with a gun, who she assumed was Clay.

At Clay's feet, she saw Derek, and her eyes welled up. Her boyfriend *was* alive but in the grips of a man with a gun and beat up to the point that he was almost unrecognizable. She thought she saw one of his hands in a cast too. Her muscles twitched and locked up as she held back from springing toward him.

Shirley and Ayla kept moving forward, hiding behind the scattered furniture and debris, and they made their way to within a city block of the arguing men in the center.

"That's Clay," Ayla whispered and pointed to the man with the gun.

Shirley's mouth opened, and she nodded in agreement.

"He has Derek," she whispered again, her voice barely audible. "I have to save him."

Shirley gripped Ayla's forearms and shook her head.

"I have to."

Shirley held up one finger.

Ayla sighed. Thoughts of how to save Derek and how to save everyone else, like Shirley and those back at the pond, flew through her head. The little girl with ponytails from the hallway popped in and out of focus. Her mind pounded, and she shook her head, like she was trying to clear up the picture on an old TV. She slouched closer to the floor and heard Clay's voice ring out.

"Down to fifteen minutes."

A time limit? On what?

"Time is getting precious," he called out again and lowered his gun to Derek's head.

Shit.

Shirley put her hand up to Ayla's mouth. Ayla must have said it out loud. "Sorry," she whispered.

"You know, Clay, I thought you might change over the years." Lee was talking now and walking toward Clay with Thomas closely in tow behind him.

"Careful, old man." Clay pointed the gun at Lee, who stopped in his tracks. Thomas stopped too. "I'm not here for you." He paused. "Yet." He pulled the gun down and pointed it back at Derek, whose head was now stooped below his shoulders.

"Same tactics too, I see." Lee inched forward with an eye on Clay's gun.

"I don't want to fight," Clay said. "I really don't. It's been a busy week."

"I'm not here to fight either," Lee said.

"The only reason you're here is to tell me where Ayla is, and if you can't do that, I might as well shoot you now."

"I don't know where she is, Clay."

"Well then *his* blood"—Clay motioned to Derek—"will be on your hands."

"I just want everyone here to be safe." Lee raised his head, speaking to everyone leaning over the railings and walkways above. Ayla assumed he was trying to convince the neutral towns-people he was a good guy. She wasn't so sure herself, but now, see-ing Clay, she knew Lee had to be better than him.

"I can't have people from the outside roaming free around here."

"They haven't caused any trouble," Lee said.

"I don't think my boss would see it that way." Spittle flew from the corners of Clay's mouth.

The action continued to unfold in front of Ayla, giving her little time to reflect on anything.

"I don't know how your boss would see it, but I know they wouldn't be too fond of anyone dying unnecessarily, right?"

"He doesn't care." Clay trained the gun on Lee, who raised his hands and pointed his palms at Clay.

"I told you, I'm not here to cause problems," Lee said.

"Too late," Clay said, jabbing his gun in the air to emphasize his words. "You're causing problems by not telling me where I can find Ayla. She's a spy, Lee. She's here to help the enemy."

"I know that's not true." Lee inched forward and Thomas fol-lowed alongside him.

"What would you know?" Clay asked.

"You're holding us hostage here," Lee said.

"You have no proof," Clay argued.

"If they were spies, why wouldn't you have killed him already?" Lee pointed at Derek.

"Live bait is always better."

Ayla ducked her head back behind the decrepit couch and held her breath. She closed her eyes. Her body shook and fought the battle of whether to flee or fight. She focused first on her hands, calming them down, stopping the shaking, and then took another deep breath and opened her eyes. "You stay here," she told Shirley. "No matter what happens, okay?"

Shirley's eyes widened, and her lips turned as pale as the rest of her face. She reluctantly nodded.

Ayla turned back to the chaos. Beside the couch was a broken pipe. She picked it up, crouched, and snuck forward, keeping her body low to the ground and weaving in and out of kiosks and tents and tipped-over chairs. She stepped over food scraps, leftovers, trash, and broken mugs dropped by those people hurriedly flee-ing the scene she was now heading straight for. She crept up to-ward the guard closest to her, trying not to become distracted by the back-and-forth banter happening in the middle of the room. Gripping the pipe and holding it out at waist level, she tiptoed closer to the guard.

She got to within arm's length and held out her pipe, jamming it into the guard's back. "Don't move," she whispered. "Give me your weapon." She eyed the guard as his hand slowly moved to his hip. His fingers twitched, and Ayla wasn't sure what she would do if he tried to fight, but luckily, she didn't have to figure it out, as he reached for his holster, removed his gun, and handed it to Ayla. "Drop to your knees." The guard followed her directions and Ayla's attention went back to the scene in the middle of the room.

"What if *I'm* a spy, Clay?" Lee shouted now. "What if none of this is real?"

"What are you talking about? You've always been crazy. Your sidekick too." Clay lowered his gun and squared up to the men ap-proaching him. "You want me to kill you both?"

If Ayla was a better shot, she'd take aim for Clay, but she wasn't going to risk injuring Derek or any innocent bystanders. She tucked her newly acquired gun into her pants. Clay was distracted, and it was now or never. Ayla took off, sprinting toward Clay and Derek. Her mind went on pause, like a movie in the middle of an action scene. She sensed her body moving but no longer felt in control. Her legs strained and bulged with every step. Her arms swung in slow motion. The ground below her turned into a blur as her vision tunneled in on Clay and Derek.

She was halfway to Clay.

The disarmed guard behind her shouted something.

Clay turned his head, still pointing his gun at Lee and Thomas.

Ayla wasn't sure if her feet were touching the ground anymore.

Clay turned his hips to bring the gun toward Ayla.

Derek swung his handcuffed arms and smashed them into Clay's kneecaps.

Clay crumpled to the ground.

His gun fired, and a bullet ricocheted off the floor.

There were loud screams.

Ayla kept pumping her legs.

Clay was half-kneeling on the ground now and looked up again right as Ayla slammed into him, shoulder-first, knocking him backward. Out of her peripheral vision, Thomas sprinted toward guard number two, who lined up to take aim at Ayla. Thomas and the second guard fell to the ground in a struggle. Lee took off running and flew past Ayla, presumably to take care of the first guard Ayla had passed. She dropped her knee onto Clay's throat, leaving him gagging for air, and grabbed the pistol from her pants, smashing it into his forehead, and pointed the barrel at his temple.

"Throw your weapon away," she screamed.

Clay's face turned red, and his eyes bulged. He hastily tossed his weapon aside, feet from where he was struggling to breathe. Ayla put more pressure on Clay's throat, almost to the point of crushing his windpipe. Derek's insistence on teaching her strong self-defense maneuvers was finally paying off. Ayla couldn't see the other struggles, but Lee shortly found his way to Ayla and Clay with a set of handcuffs. He locked Clay's hands together.

"Got these off the guard," Lee said.

Ayla glanced over to see the guard knocked out on the floor, close to where she had left him in the first place.

"I can take him," Lee said, pointing at Clay. He had picked up Clay's discarded gun, and Ayla stood up, glad to let Lee take over watch for her. She went to Derek and threw her arms around him, and he fell into her. A giant sigh escaped her lips, and tears rolled down her cheeks. She swore that a faint hint of his cologne hit her nostrils, but it was likely all in her head. Either way, she didn't care. She ran her fingers through his hair and remembered the all-too-familiar feeling.

"I missed you so much." She drew her tear-streaked face back and looked him in the eyes. She ran a finger over the biggest bruise on his face.

Derek opened his mouth. "Where's the other guard?" his weak voice whispered.

"Thomas!" Lee cried out from on top of Clay.

Ayla snapped out of the moment and turned in time to see the guard knock Thomas to the ground. There was a struggle, and the guard jumped back up with a gun in his hand. He fired it once at Thomas, hitting him in the shoulder, who then lay motionless on the floor.

"No!" Ayla screamed. She popped up, pointed the gun at the

guard, and fired off as many shots as she could until the trigger clicked.

All of her shots missed.

"Ayla, no." Derek's weak voice wavered from his position on the floor.

Lee pointed his own gun at the guard who had shot Thomas. Lee's arm shook, and the gun waved back and forth between the guard and Clay.

Clay started laughing from the floor. "Bravo," he said. "Looks like we have a good old-fashioned standoff."

The guard, with his sights still on Lee, circled the group to head over to the other stunned guard. Lee's gun followed the guard the entire way, occasionally pointing back to Clay, who was restrained on the ground.

"You know you can't win," Clay said.

Lee stood in the center of the action, shaking. His beard, bunched up in knots like he had just rolled out of bed, waved back and forth. His eyes were bloodshot, and his legs started to buckle. Tears fell off his nose and splatted against the floor.

"Lee, don't do it. You can't give up, not now," Ayla pleaded. Lee's face was more sunken now, his nose overtaking the rest of his face, which was now flush, and his cheeks were red. His eyes started twitching.

"I'm sorry, Ayla." He lowered his gun and dropped it to the floor. The gun-less guard scrambled to grab it and pointed it directly at Lee's head.

"Lee, no!" Ayla yelled.

The other guard ran over and put Ayla in a chokehold. She screamed and kicked her legs, trying to free herself. The guard had a vise-like grip on her throat, and the more she struggled, the more it felt like she was choking herself. Derek, still handcuffed, squirmed on the floor and tried to put up a fight, but the first guard was quick to step on his abdomen and pin him against the floor.

Clay stood up. One of the guards unlocked his handcuffs.

"Now, where were we?" Clay asked, rubbing his wrists.

"You know, it really is a shame," Clay said as he walked behind the guards who had their guns pointed straight ahead at Derek, Ayla, and Lee. "I thought you might put up more of a fight than that. It's okay. Nothing another fifteen years can't solve." He laughed in an unusual way.

Ayla looked at the men next to her. They hobbled forward, hanging their heads, as defeated as anyone she had ever seen. The entire weight of the world and everyone's hopes were pinned again on Ayla's shoulders. She plodded along, close to giving in to defeat. She leaned into Derek and rested her head on his shoulder, another long-forgotten feeling. This time seemed like it might be the last.

"Remember our friend the pit, Derek?" Clay kicked Derek in the back of the legs. Ayla grabbed at her boyfriend with her restrained hands and tried to support him as he stumbled forward.

"Hey—" Ayla was cut off by a noise coming from behind the group. From the bottom of the tower in the middle of the room, a door opened, and Katherine appeared, handcuffed, with Jeffrey close behind her. One of the guards held up his gun and pointed it at them.

"Wait!" Clay shouted.

Katherine grimaced and shuffled forward.

Jeffrey spoke up. "I tried to stop her . . ."

"Jeff," Clay said. "I didn't think you had it in you." He walked toward Katherine, who fought and wriggled against Jeffrey's grip. "Like you're serving her up on a platter." Clay reached out and grabbed her cuffed wrists. He pulled out a black rectangular device from his back pocket and jammed it into her arm. A spark flew from the device, and Katherine went limp. Clay dragged her over to the rest of the group and tossed her on the floor.

Clay sized up Jeffrey. There was a brief silence before Clay finally said, "Thanks. Can you check Thomas over there?" He pointed off to the body lying motionless on the ground, surrounded by a spreading puddle of blood. "He might not be okay."

"You *monster*," Lee blurted out. His face was red now, glowing like a hot iron. Sweat and tears gleamed on his cheeks. He had to be pulled back by the guard.

Clay stopped within inches of Lee's face and leaned in. "This is on *you*. You pushed over that first domino."

Jeffrey walked over to where Thomas was, and Katherine slowly came to and got up on all fours. Ayla had a hard time reconciling the events unfolding in front of her. Thomas was on the floor, left for dead, Lee was a shell of his former self, sobbing and shaking, and Derek stood in place, swaying back and forth. Everything around her was falling apart. She had to come up with a new plan, but the nightmarish situation around her made it hard to focus.

"He's breathing!" Jeffrey called out from behind the table.

Clay sighed. "Take him to the hospital and deal with him there."

Lee tried to get a look at Thomas, who was now slung over Jeffrey's shoulder.

"Show him some respect!" Lee cried out. A guard hit him in the side with the butt of his gun and Lee doubled over.

"And thank you for your help," Clay said to Jeffrey, who now headed toward the hospital. "I'll remember that when I come back."

Jeffrey faced Clay. "Thank *you*," he said and continued toward the hospital.

"Now, about that pit," Clay said, addressing the group. "Shall we?" He gestured forward.

"The pit?" Katherine asked. "I thought that was a myth." She stood now, but like a newborn, she bobbed from side to side and tried to catch her balance.

"Well, Kate," Clay spat, "you tell me when we get down there. If it doesn't totally rip you to shreds and kill you, good news, it is a myth!"

The guards corralled everyone back to the main walkway and headed for the elevator. Ayla reminded herself to breathe in through her nose and out through her mouth. Rhythmic breathing. It kept her focused.

Feeling lightheaded and tired, she was worried she'd pass out or be unable to keep reality straight. The breathing was the only thing keeping her centered. She tried not to panic. Panic was the last thing anyone needed now.

"You know, I'm going to miss this," Clay said.

"Shut up, Clay," Katherine said weakly.

Clay kicked her in the back of the legs and she stumbled forward. "Next time, you'll get stunned again. Keep moving."

Derek groaned, and Ayla tried to reach her handcuffed hands to his. Their fingertips touched. She tried to focus on their comfortable bed back at home, snuggling on the couch with Bella, laughing with friends at dinner, having a barbecue on the roof, but nothing could distract her enough—nothing could pull her mind entirely away from the situation at hand.

She tried to focus on her mother and sharing a last meal with her, as well as the very faint, distant memories of her father, wishing that, somehow, he would be able to appear from nowhere and rescue her.

She missed her old struggles.

She missed her simple problems.

She missed her boring life.

And now she might not see it again.

The bell on the elevator dinged, and the group stepped forward and waited for the doors.

Clay started talking again. "You know, there are only—"

He was cut off by a loud popping sound, followed by a rapid fire of others. One of the guards dropped to the floor, and the other crouched and ran off to find cover. Clay scrambled for something to hide behind. Lee, Derek, Katherine, and Ayla were caught in the crossfire.

Ayla grabbed and threw Derek down, lying on top of him. There was noise and chaos, but she wasn't going to lose Derek again. She clung to his shirt as tightly as she could. The elevator doors opened farther, and two figures appeared: a woman and a man— the same man who had yelled at her right before she jumped into Shirley's room in the lower levels. The two stood tall inside the elevator doors, guns drawn, shooting at Clay and his guards.

"Get in here!" the woman screamed at the group, above the noise.

Ayla yanked Derek off the floor, lowered her shoulder, and

drove them both forward. They passed Katherine and Lee, who still appeared confused. Ayla tried to reach out and grab them too, but with her restraints, she was limited, and she wasn't going to slow down. She pushed until she and Derek were in the elevator and fell into the far corner. When they landed, Ayla stayed in front of him and turned.

"Come on!" Ayla shouted toward Katherine and Lee, who finally started to run toward the elevator. They reached the inside while getting cover from the man and woman. Once safely inside, Katherine and Lee dropped to the elevator floor.

The woman crouched down with the group. "Stay down," she said.

The man turned his attention to the buttons on the side and slammed something into the slot where the S button used to be.

As the feeling of safety and comfort started to wash over Ayla, Clay appeared at the open elevator doors and held one hand up against them so they wouldn't close. The other hand held a gun and pointed it squarely at the back of the woman's head.

"Ellen—" Katherine shouted and pointed toward the door.

A blur came from outside the elevator door and slammed into Clay's side. As if in slow motion, Clay flew out of Ayla's line of sight.

And then Ayla realized who the blur was.

"No!" She tried to stand up and scramble out of the elevator, but Derek held her back. All she could do was reach her hands out as the doors closed. "Shirley!"

TWENTY

Homebound

Ayla was numb.

Her body tingled.

She couldn't feel her hands, and her gut twisted into a ball.

She stared ahead at the closed doors and sat in silence as the elevator hummed downward. Shirley sacrificed everything, potentially her life, so they could escape. This woman she hardly knew had risked everything. Ayla was frozen stiff, unable to comprehend what was happening.

Ellen and the strange man were ready again with their weapons, the rest of the group quiet. Katherine sat against the wall, mostly stoic, but with a thousand-yard stare off into the distance. Lee did mostly the same, whimpering every now and again. Ayla leaned on Derek, and the two huddled together.

The past few minutes had seemed like a dream.

Eventually, Katherine broke the silence. "What's going on?" she asked as the elevator clunked onward.

"We're getting out of here," Ellen replied.

"And who are you?" Ayla asked.

"Doesn't matter."

Ayla didn't care to ask a follow-up question.

The strange man now lowered his gun and held out his hand. "I'm Sam," he said. "Sorry about earlier. I think there was a . . . misunderstanding. We . . . We needed your help."

"You were the one chasing me in the lower levels, weren't you?" Ayla asked. "You were calling out my name?"

"Yes, ma'am."

"And you needed my help?"

"Yes, that's correct."

"How could I possibly help you?" she asked.

He paused, swallowed, and licked his lips. He turned to Ellen, who nodded slightly. "To escape."

Ayla squinted. Sam wasn't any more trustworthy than anyone else she was around. "What do you mean?" she asked.

"There's an escape plan, in the case of an emergency," Ellen butted in. "And we're using it."

Lee suddenly perked up in the corner. "An escape plan?"

"Is that your group?" Ayla asked Lee.

"Your group?" Katherine asked. "The *faction*?"

Ayla turned back to Ellen. "Were you there at the lake?"

Ellen sneered at Lee. "I *knew* the faction was still around." She kicked the side of the elevator.

"Ellen, I didn't know," Katherine said.

"Yeah, right," Ellen replied.

Katherine looked back to Lee. "Why didn't you tell me?"

Lee shrugged and raised his eyebrows.

"Look," Ayla interrupted, "I have no idea what the hell is going on, but can you at least get us out of these handcuffs?"

Ellen stood up and walked around to Ayla, glaring at Lee and Katherine the whole time. "Spread out your arms," Ellen directed. "And put the cuffs flat against the floor."

Ayla spread out her handcuffs and put them as flat as possible on the floor of the elevator.

"Everyone, brace yourselves." Ellen lined her sights up with the cuffs on the floor, and as everyone leaned away from Ayla and covered their heads, Ellen fired. A bright-blue burst of light shot out from the barrel of her weapon. A *crack* rang out in the tiny space, and the edges of Ayla's handcuffs disintegrated. Ayla flinched backward, once again finding herself in the middle of a science fiction dream. A faint "whoa" came from her mouth. The elevator clanged against something, distracting Ayla and sending everyone onto all fours.

After regaining her balance, Ellen aimed her sights at Derek's handcuffs. "Your turn."

Another bright-blue beam of light shot out of Ellen's weapon, and the moment he was free, Ayla ran to him, and they threw their arms around each other. Ayla pulled back and mouthed, "I love you."

There was another burst of blue light when Katherine had her cuffs removed, but Ayla didn't pay attention; she was busy taking in all that she could in the moment. She no longer knew how many more moments existed.

"Why did you . . . come down here?" Derek asked. His voice was still raspy, and his face glistened from bruises.

"I'm sorry." It was all she could think to say. She started crying. "I'm the only reason we're in this mess."

"It's okay," Derek said, pulling her in more closely. "We'll get out of here."

"But there are others," she said.

"I think we're almost there," Ellen interrupted.

"I'm not leaving without everyone else," Lee said abruptly, standing up to face the rest of the group.

The doors started to open.

"I can't leave everyone else behind."

"He's right," Ayla said. "There are so many others here who need our help."

"Look," Ellen said. "You're lucky enough I stopped to save *you*."

Katherine perked up. "Why *did* you stop to save us?"

"We don't have the manpower to go back for everyone anyway," Ellen said, ignoring Katherine's question.

"She's right," Derek said, standing up next to Ayla. "We would just be going on a suicide mission."

"We can't leave everyone else in the hands of Clay, can we?" Lee asked. "Just imagine what he's going to do."

"My gut tells me his top priority now is finding us," Ellen said. "And until we're safe, there's no way in hell you can save everyone else."

Ayla knew the logic was sound, and there was no way to reasonably save everyone now, but it tugged at her and bothered her more than anything else ever had. If she turned back around, she could be causing even more pain, like what she had done to Derek and everyone in this elevator. She closed her eyes and looked down.

"We have to come back," she said.

"We will," Derek whispered.

"Can we talk about this later?" Ellen interrupted again. "Clay's going to be right behind us."

"She's right," Katherine said. "Unfortunately."

"Stay behind me," Ellen said, taking a step out beyond the elevator doors. "Sam will take the back."

The group poured out of the confined elevator, Ellen first, then Katherine and Lee, followed by Ayla and Derek, with Sam bringing up the rear.

"Where are we?" Katherine asked quietly. Her words echoed off the smooth walls, which ran two stories high and as far ahead as Ayla could make out.

"Subfloor section," Sam said from the back.

"I think I was just here . . ." Derek said softly.

"What?" Ayla asked.

"They were keeping you down here?" Katherine asked.

"Impossible," Ellen said. "Most of this was closed off when we introduced portals."

"I swear it was here. I don't know . . . exactly where, but I remember the elevator."

"The only thing down here are supplies," Ellen added.

"Clay does have access though, right?" Katherine chimed in.

"Let's just keep going." Ellen pushed her way farther ahead.

Eventually, they were forced into a single-file line, squeezing together as the hallway narrowed. The farther they got down the hall, the more it was filled with tubes and pipes and wires running every which way, like a rat's nest, as if someone had thrown everything around and left it where it landed. There seemed to be no rhyme or reason to this place, other than it being filled with leftover junk. The group inched forward in the landfill-like room, slowly, so as not to alarm anyone who might be watching, though Ayla had her doubts there was anyone down here at all.

"Where are we going?" Ayla asked after a few paces.

"An emergency exit," Ellen said.

"What?" Katherine asked. "There's an exit? How do you know about it?"

"Need-to-know basis," Ellen replied.

"We're part of leadership, Ellen. You didn't think we needed to know?" Lee asked.

Ellen stopped suddenly, turned around, and raised her voice. "Do you want to get out of here or not?"

The rhetorical question lingered in the air and left everyone in the group silent as they tiptoed around and through a jungle of plastics and metal, broken-off pieces of leftover supplies, and jagged chunks of discarded building materials. They stepped over *actual* garbage on the floor too, including mouse droppings and carcasses. Ayla tried to keep her shirt above her nose because the farther they went down this hallway, the more the hot smell of the bottom of a dumpster lingered in the air. The stench was somehow worse than the stairs she took to get to this place.

"We've got to be there soon, right?" Ayla asked through her old shirt.

"We're looking for a vault door of some kind," Ellen said, lifting her gun and pushing dangling wires out of her line of vision.

The group continued walking, and Ayla kept her eyes peeled. She expected to see an old-style bank-vault type of door, a large chunk of metal that would take two people to swing open, and maybe a large spinning wheel in the middle to unlock it. Ellen wasn't much farther ahead now, but she stopped and held up her hand to indicate the group should stop as well.

"What is it?" Lee asked.

"It's nothing," she said, turning back to the group.

Sam kept climbing through the maze, moving forward in the group until he stood next to Ellen, who inspected the wall in front of them.

"Then let's keep going," Katherine insisted.

"No, I mean it's nothing. There's nothing here," Ellen said.

"It's just a wall," Sam said.

Sam and Ellen stood in front of the group now, feeling the wall, trying to find weaknesses, while the rest of the group huddled together. Ayla wasn't sure she could help, but it didn't seem like a good sign that they had now cornered themselves in a small, narrow hallway.

"Dammit!" Ellen yelled. Her voice bounced around the walls and through the trash. She turned to the rest of the group. "Go back." She motioned with her hand and started trudging through the group.

"That's it?" Ayla asked. "There's nothing here?"

"I told you," Ellen said as she passed Ayla and headed back to where the group had come from, "it was probably sealed off or removed when we introduced portals."

"Can't we *unseal* it?" Lee asked.

"Yeah, you're just going to give up?" Ayla rushed forward and smashed her hands into the wall. It had to be here somewhere. It wouldn't have just disappeared.

"Ayla?" Derek stepped forward.

"We came all this way, right? We can't just stop," Ayla said.

"We don't have any tools," Ellen said. "And we don't have much time."

"But Ayla's right." Katherine stepped forward and helped Ayla search the wall. "If we stop now, we have failed everyone who has helped us get here and everyone we are coming back to save."

"*We*?" Ellen asked sarcastically. "*You* may be coming back, Katherine, but I hope to never see this place again."

"Have some empathy for once, Ellen," Lee said, joining the group against the far wall.

"Can I remind you," Ellen said, "that we have a literal madman chasing us?"

"I think we need to go," Derek said, stepping away from Ayla and the others. "If I know Clay, he won't be too far behind us." He paused to take a deep breath. "And if we can't get out, we're going to be trapped here."

"He's right," Sam said.

Ayla stopped clawing at the wall and turned to find her boyfriend suddenly siding with Ellen and Sam. "Derek, we can't give up."

"I'm not saying to give up." He turned to Ellen. "You have a backup plan, don't you?"

"There's another door leading to the outside."

Lee and Katherine stopped rummaging around the wall. "Supplies," Katherine said.

Ellen nodded. "It's the only other way anything gets in or out. Clay uses it. It's how I talk to him. Or used to talk to him."

She kicked a piece of trash away from her leg. "It's our only way out now."

"Clay will know that too, right?" Lee said.

"All the more reason to get there before he does." Ellen headed back from where they had come. "That's where I'm going," Ellen repeated, this time more annoyed than before.

Ayla took a deep breath and kept her shirt above her nose. The second-to-last thing she wanted to do was trek through the dumpster pile again. The last thing she wanted to do was stay there like sitting ducks, and Derek had come to that conclusion well before her. They walked back through the garbage- and trash-infested hallway until they reached the elevator again and turned left. Not far away from the elevator was a door marked with "WW-2."

"One of the originals," Katherine said.

Ellen went up to the door and swiped her keycard. The door slid open, revealing a familiar red, gooey substance.

"This was one of the first places we installed wall walkers. Supply room is right on the other side. Thought it'd be a good test." She stepped into the goo and disappeared. Sam followed shortly after.

"Looks like this is our only option." Katherine held Lee's hand and dragged him into the goo behind her.

Ayla reached down and grabbed Derek's hand, and without saying anything, she led him through the wall walker.

Ayla's head pounded again when she reached the other side, and she had to block her eyes from a bright light coming from above. The room was the size of a three-car garage and three times as high. The bright halogen lights bounced off the polished concrete floor. There were boxes and crates stacked high throughout and only one table and chair close to them. A giant welded-shut door occupied the entire far wall of the room.

"This is it?" Katherine asked no one in particular.

"What now?" Ayla asked, her headache starting to subside.

"The external door," Ellen said, examining a door next to the one Ayla had just come through. "This is the portal Clay uses to come down here. I've seen him leave this way, but I don't know how to get out . . ." She approached the sturdy metal door.

"Didn't your team build these?" Katherine asked.

"Clay had outside help with these, and I don't know how they were modified, but they're not exactly like ours. They don't even have keycard access." She held out her card and swiped it all over the door, which remained still. Sam came over and tried swiping his in different spots.

The elevator came to life, and the thick clunking sound echoed throughout the room.

"Can't you figure out how to open it?" Katherine pressed. "Isn't that your job?"

"Let me think!" Ellen yelled. "Would you like to help or just fight about it?"

"I don't know anything about them," Katherine replied.

"Well, if anyone has any ideas, I'd like to hear them. Otherwise, be quiet . . ." Ellen turned her attention back to the door.

"I have an idea." Derek's voice was soft and mostly inaudible.

"What is it?" Ayla asked him. She looked around the rest of the group. "I think Derek knows something."

"What?" Ellen asked, her focus stuck on the door.

"When they brought me up here from that prison cell"—Derek licked his lips—"we went through a portal. But it didn't open right away, and Clay said something about . . . jamming." His voice got stronger, and he stopped and took a deep breath. "I didn't see what *exactly* it was, but one of the guards shoved . . ." Ayla nodded at him in encouragement. "He shoved *something* between the door and the wall to open it."

Ayla's brain clicked, and another piece of the puzzle jumped out to her. "I saw that work too," she said. "When I got down here from the abandoned building, I couldn't get past that WW-8 door, so I slammed my crowbar down, and it was stuck between the door and the floor. The next thing I knew, the door is open and I could get through. It must have short-circuited the connection or something."

"Impossible," Ellen said. "This technology can't be worked around like that. We have restrictions and safety checks and—"

"But it worked," Ayla said.

"It's worth a shot," Lee added.

The elevator clunked away in the distance.

"Give me your keycard." Ayla turned to Katherine. She grabbed the card from Katherine's hands and scrambled to the door.

"It's not going to work," Ellen said, stepping back.

"I have to try." Ayla jammed the card between the door and the wall, but nothing happened.

"I told you," Ellen said. "We'll guard the doors. Maybe we'll get lucky. Sam, help me." They walked over to one of the closest crates. "Get behind here," she said, directing the rest of the group, all of whom had transformed into spectators.

"Wait," Ayla said.

"Ayla . . ." Derek said.

"I think I can get it." She angled the card so it bent slightly and touched both the door and the wall at the same time. The minute she made contact with the wall, the door flew upward and disappeared. Ayla again faced a wall of red goo that shone and reflected the lights above. "Let's go," Ayla said, stepping back and motioning to the rest of the group.

"I don't like this," Lee said.

"Lee, we'll come back, okay?" Ayla assured him. "Right, Katherine?" Ayla knew Katherine the best out of everyone down here, and she tried to play into her reassuring instincts. If she could get Katherine on her side, Lee would have to join them.

"Yes," Katherine said after a brief pause. "Lee, if we go back now, we're not going to be able to help anyone, including Thomas. You understand that, right?"

Lee sniffled and wiped tears away from his face. "Promise me we'll come back."

Both Ayla and Katherine nodded.

"Let's go!" Ellen said, now standing by the open portal. "We'll go first. We have weapons." She turned to face the wall and pushed Sam in front of her. "Ready?" she asked. Sam stepped forward and disappeared into the goo. Ellen followed quickly behind.

Katherine took Lee's hand and led him to the portal. She turned back to Ayla and Derek. "Don't wait too long." Both her and Lee disappeared into the portal.

"You okay?" Derek whispered, turning to Ayla.

He was always the first to catch her if something was bothering her. "I'm fine," she lied. "Let's go."

She didn't feel like explaining it all right now. It was difficult for her brain to reconcile leaving behind good people trapped in a not-so-good place. Her childhood flashed before her. If she hadn't escaped her hometown, she could only imagine how much worse her life would be at the moment.

She thought about the people by the pond.

She thought about Shirley.

She thought about Thomas.

What would happen to them?

Derek led her to the front of the portal, and as they got closer, her arm tensed up. She jolted Derek to a stop.

"I can't do this," she whispered.

"Why?" Derek stepped back and picked up Ayla's other hand with his cast.

"I just . . . I just can't leave these people behind."

The elevator noises stopped. Derek's glance darted to the entryway door.

"Ayla, this is not a good place." He swallowed hard, and his eyes hid more pain behind the bruises and scrapes on his face. He spoke with a sense of urgency and held up his bandaged hand. "There are *bad* people here—"

"You didn't see what I saw. We didn't experience the same place."

"We can't save everyone," he said. "Yet."

"We can at least try."

"We'll come back, just like you said," Derek said. "You, me, Katherine, Lee, maybe others. We'll be stronger." He licked his lips. "We'll come back, okay?"

Ayla stared into his eyes, and a sense of partnership and trust washed over her. A feeling she had missed the entire time she was here. Even if no one else wanted to see this place again, Derek's words rang as true as ever.

"But right now," Derek continued, "we have to leave. We have to help ourselves . . . before we can help the others." He turned to face the glowing red portal. Ayla's arms loosened, and she stepped forward to join him. "Whatever happens, I love you." He leaned in and kissed her.

They both walked forward into the portal.

Acknowledgments

Many people helped along the way, and I'd like to thank them here. I can't possibly provide enough thanks to my editors, who helped take my pile of garbage and make something fantastic out of it. Thank you to Melissa Jackson, Courtney Andersson of Elevation Editorial, Tim Marquitz, and Bodie Dykstra. Thank you also to my designer Ben Mcleod, who made my vision for the underground world come to life. A special thanks also goes out to Nick Castle, for the additional design work, and Bryan Cohen.

I also would not have been able to get through this book without the understanding and loving support of my family: Karla, Aizlynn, Emery, Friley, and Charley!

CPSIA information can be obtained
at www.ICGtesting.com
Printed in the USA
FSHW012354300420
69765FS

9 780984 309634